Changes Afoot

'Here are the letters ready to sign, Michael.' Kay laid the documents on her boss's desk and turned to leave.

'Kay, would you tell everyone that we'd like them in my office at three?'

'Yes, of course, but did you know Charlie hasn't turned up today? We haven't heard anything from him, but I suppose he's ill.'

Michael Harris's face was grim.

'I know he isn't in. He left us yesterday. That will be all, Kay, thank you.'

Kay wasn't used to him being anything other than friendly and kind to her and was surprised at how upset she felt that he had spoken so sharply. She wondered if running the busy solicitor's office was going to be too much for him when his father retired.

She sighed as she sat down at her

own desk and sorted through the papers on it. Michael was a very attractive man with his boyish good looks, his blond hair constantly flopping down over his bright blue eyes. Not only was he attractive, he was also very fair and supportive to his staff. Since she'd been working for him they'd built up a very good relationship and she almost regarded him as a friend.

She and Mr Harris senior's secretary were the only two members of staff who knew he was retiring early due to ill health and she imagined the meeting was to announce this.

Suddenly she remembered Michael had asked her to tell everyone about the meeting. It was most unlike her not to be the height of efficiency, and as she scurried round she wondered why she had been so distracted, just because Michael had been curt with her.

She returned once more to her desk, settling herself in front of her typewriter to begin transcribing her shorthand notes. Michael popped his

TIME AFTER TIME

When Kay falls in love with Michael, her boss, she thinks he will always put his business first. Together they discover there are plans to discredit the company, so they set out to expose those responsible. Kay hopes the excellent working relationship they have will overflow into their personal lives, and wishes she knew Michael's feelings for her. In the 1950s it isn't easy to ask. Can she fly in the face of convention?

Books by Patricia Keyson
in the Linford Romance Library:

CHERRY BLOSSOM

PATRICIA KEYSON

◆

TIME AFTER TIME

Complete and Unabridged

LINFORD
Leicester

First published in Great Britain in 2012

First Linford Edition
published 2013

A catalogue record for this book is available
from the British Library.

ISBN 978–1–4448–1684–6

Published by
F. A. Thorpe (Publishing)
Anstey, Leicestershire

Set by Words & Graphics Ltd.
Anstey, Leicestershire
Printed and bound in Great Britain by
T. J. International Ltd., Padstow, Cornwall

This book is printed on acid-free paper

head round the door.

'My office, please, Kay.'

When she walked in he was standing at the window gazing out at the street. He turned.

'Take a seat. I'm sorry I was short with you. As you know, I have rather a lot on my mind at the moment, but that doesn't excuse my behaviour. Forgive me?'

Kay smiled. He looked rather like a puppy with his wistful expression.

'You're the boss, you can be however you want to be. There's nothing to forgive.'

Michael sat down on the other side of the desk.

'Let's agree to disagree on that one. I'm afraid there's going to be a lot more pressure when Dad retires. I think he's already having doubts about going and leaving things in my hands. I'm determined to prove I'm up to the job. It's quite an undertaking and I'll need everyone's support. I hope that you're prepared to take on a bigger workload.'

Kay was always extremely busy and wasn't quite sure how she'd manage even more work, but she was willing.

'I'll do my best. What will Mr Harris do when he retires?'

'Take it easy, I hope. He and Mum want to travel. They're talking about Scotland first whilst the weather's good and maybe France next year. Dad's keen to take up bird-watching. That minor heart attack had us all scared and Mum wants them to celebrate their golden wedding. Some years to go, of course.'

Kay wondered how old Michael was. Definitely in his early thirties. She didn't know much about his family except that he was an only child, and she'd heard that he'd always been expected to join the family business. Not that he'd ever seemed unhappy.

'I'm thirty-two, if that's what you were wondering. They've been married for thirty-three years.

Kay giggled. It was funny how often he could read her mind.

'Will there be many changes?'

'Quite a few. Some will be pretty major and some of the staff may not like it.'

'So that's why Charlie left. You told him your plans.' As soon as she'd spoken she wished the words back in her mouth.

'No. I have never confided in Charlie. He's gone now and I don't want to think of him.'

Once again Michael looked tense and angry. For some reason any mention of his male accounts clerk changed his mood completely. Kay was curious to know what was behind his anger. Maybe it involved a woman.

'Where will you go when you retire?'

Michael laughed.

'Distraction isn't one of your strong points, is it? I haven't given it any thought. Have you?'

'I'm only twenty!'

Kay felt more content now the tension between them had disappeared. She watched the clock on the wall drawing towards three.

'Betty,' she said to the most junior member of staff, 'could you make the tea a little earlier than usual, please? I think we could put it on the trolley and wheel it into Mr Michael's office.'

Kay had a feeling they were all going to need a cuppa to arm them against the news Michael was about to impart. She watched as Betty filled the sugar bowl.

'It's so nice to be off rationing and have as much sugar as we like, isn't it?'

Betty grinned.

'Mr Michael has loads of sugar in his tea. I suppose that's where he gets all his energy from.' Her face clouded over. 'I wonder why we've got to see him.'

Nervously, the employees of Harris and Son followed Kay as she wheeled the tea trolley towards the office.

'Good idea,' Michael whispered, indicating the cups and saucers as he opened the door in answer to her knock.

Betty fussed around, pouring tea,

adding milk and sugar and carrying cups and saucers to people. Mr Robert Harris took his cup gratefully and sipped at the hot liquid. The staff had taken their seats and were nursing their cups. The air was expectant as they waited to hear why they'd been summoned.

Michael stood up, put his cup on his desk and spoke.

'It must be a bit of a shock for you all to have been asked to attend a meeting with us, but there's nothing to worry about,' he assured them.

There was an audible sigh from his audience.

'Dad and I . . . ' Mr Harris senior cleared his throat and Michael looked in his direction. He grinned and continued, 'Mr Harris and I have something to tell you. He has decided that it is time for him to retire from the practice.' He paused so they could take in what he was saying. 'I have been invited to take the reins and I hope you won't be too disappointed with that arrangement.'

'I'll be very happy to work with you in charge, Mr Michael,' Betty piped up. 'But I'll miss Mr Harris.' She fished up her sleeve for a handkerchief and dabbed at her eyes.

Mr Harris senior gave the young girl a smile.

'Thank you, Betty. I'll miss you, too, as well as the rest of the first-rate team we've been so lucky to have here. But the time has come for me to stand aside and let my son be in charge. I'm sure he'll do a good job, particularly if you all decide you'll stay on with him after I've left.'

Kay listened to what was being said with a thumping heart. What did he mean by that? Why wouldn't they stay? What could happen to make them even think about leaving? She glanced around the room wondering if anyone else had similar thoughts, but if they did, their faces showed no curiosity.

Michael's father continued.

'I won't be leaving immediately as I

have a few things to settle first, but I wanted you all to know the news. One important item I have to tell you is that, in recognition of your loyalty, there will be a bonus lump sum paid to each of you.'

Happy smiles were now on the faces of the employees as they turned to each other and expressed their delight. Kay could keep quiet no longer. She stood up and the room fell quiet.

'Mr Harris, on behalf of us all here may I offer our best wishes to you and Mrs Harris and our thanks for your generosity.'

He acknowledged Kay's words with a nod.

'What about Charlie?' Betty said. 'He's not in today. How can we let him know the news?'

Kay could see Michael's jaw tightening.

'I think we can leave that to Mr Harris to deal with, Betty.' She glanced at Michael and his father and received a tight smile from Michael. 'If you'll collect the crockery, Betty, I'll help you take the trolley back.'

As the meeting broke up, Michael put his hand on Kay's elbow and squeezed it. She took it to be a thank you and was grateful that she'd stepped in as she did.

At last it was six o'clock and, with their desks cleared, everyone pulled on their coats and headed out of the office. Kay couldn't wait to get home and share the news. She had been bursting to tell her parents, but had been asked to keep it to herself. Her parents had met both Mr Harris and his son at a Christmas party the previous year and had agreed with Kay that they were good people to be working for.

She walked along to the corner with Betty who was still chattering away.

'Wasn't it lovely that Mr Harris said he'd miss me?' she said. 'I expect we'll get used to working for Mr Michael, don't you?'

'I'm sure we will.' Kay smiled, a warm feeling going through her. When they reached the place where their ways parted, she called, 'See you tomorrow.'

★   ★   ★

As Kay walked up the garden path and round to the back, a delicious smell of stew wafted out through the kitchen door. It was Tuesday and her mum was using up the last of the meat left from Sunday's roast.

In the kitchen Mrs Watson was busy at the sink, but looking perfectly groomed with her carefully permed hair and neat apron.

'There's tea in the pot, love.'

Kay wondered why she felt the need to tell her this, as there was always a pot of tea ready when she and her dad came home from work.

'Is Dad back?'

'Yes, he's taken his tea up to the shed. He's got some seedlings he wants to pot up.'

'I've got some news, Mum, but it'll wait until Dad's here.'

'Good news, I hope.'

'Yes, well, it's not bad. Quite exciting, really. For Michael, anyway.'

'Now, he's a nice young man. Not like some I could mention.'

'Don't start, Mum.' Kay took down a cup and saucer and poured some tea. 'Michael is nice, but he wouldn't give me a second look. Even if I was interested,' she added hastily. 'He's out of my league. No, I think he'll probably marry someone at the tennis club he belongs to.' Hoping to change the subject, she asked, 'I'll lay the table, shall I?'

'Please. Then go and call your dad. The vegetables are ready.'

Kay quickly completed her task then headed down to the bottom of the garden.

'Supper's ready,' she said pecking him on the cheek before picking up his empty cup.

'Best not be late, then.' After rubbing the dirt from his hands, Mr Watson tucked his daughter's arm through his.

They walked in companionable silence back to the house and sat down to their meal.

'Nice stew, Evelyn. That new butcher in the high street seems to know what he's doing. Much better than the old one.'

'Don't forget the old one, as you put it, helped us out during the rationing, Harry.'

'Anyway, not all change is bad, Dad. That's what I want to talk to you about. Mr Harris is retiring shortly and leaving Michael in charge.'

'I'm pleased for both Mr Harris senior and junior, but where does that leave you, love?'

'What on earth do you mean?'

'Well, you're Michael's secretary and Mr Harris has his own secretary. Surely she's not retiring as well? Won't she be the new boss's secretary? She's been there a lot longer than you.'

Kay's heart sank. She hadn't given that possibility any thought at all. Mr Harris senior's secretary had been at the dentist when the meeting was taking place and hadn't returned before the office closed. Kay wondered if she knew what the future plans were, and if so would it be indiscreet to ask her.

How silly she'd been to assume she would continue to be Michael's secretary, just because he'd told her there would be extra work. Maybe he'd said that to everyone. She might just have general duties, which would be a shame, as she did enjoy working closely with Michael.

'Don't worry.' Mr Watson leaned across and gave her arm a squeeze. 'It's not the end of the world.'

That night, Kay couldn't sleep. The moon was full and bright and shone through her thin curtains. She tossed and turned. Why hadn't she been told that she would be losing her job? Surely Michael should have had the decency to tell her yesterday before she heard from someone else at the office. Even Betty would probably know her future by now.

* * *

It was with a heavy heart that she settled at her desk the following day.

'Morning, Kay. Hope you're ready for a busy day,' Michael said cheerily as he disappeared into his office. He reappeared in the doorway. 'What's the matter? Are you ill? You look dreadful.'

'Thank you, Mr Harris, that's just what I need to hear.'

Michael walked over and sat on the desk.

'Why the formality? I thought we'd managed to get over that.' He fiddled with a pencil.

'I didn't sleep well, that's all. Now, if you wouldn't mind shifting, I'll get on.'

'I'm not moving until you tell me what the problem is. I can be very stubborn. Ask my parents.'

'I do know that. I have been your secretary for long enough.' Tears welled in her eyes as she fought to gain control of herself.

Michael thrust a neatly pressed

handkerchief in her hands.

'If you're worried about the extra work, please don't be. I realise there is a limit to what anyone can do, and I'm not some sort of draconian boss from the Victorian era.'

'I know.' Kay sniffed.

'So, come on, tell me.' Michael reached over and took her hand in his and held it gently as he stroked her fingers.

Just as Kay was about to unburden herself and confess her fear of the future, she was aware of Betty hovering nearby. She took a deep breath.

'Can I help you, Betty?'

Betty bobbed in deference to Michael and he raised his eyebrows towards Kay who couldn't help a small wobbly grin.

'Please, Kay, I'm running out of tea and the milk smells off. I brought the bottle in from the step first thing and it's in cold water in the sink as usual. What shall I do?'

Out of the corner of her eye, Kay

watched Michael discreetly retreating to his office.

'I'll give you some money out of petty cash, Betty,' she said, her equilibrium returning, 'and you can go to the shop along the road and get what you need. Please get a receipt as it will have to go through the account books.'

'Thank you, Kay. I was so worried, and everyone will want their tea at eleven.' Betty took the envelope into which Kay had pushed the money, and put on her coat.

Kay couldn't settle. She had to find out what was happening. Taking up her shorthand notebook, she tapped on Michael's office door.

'Come in,' he called. 'Ah, Kay, I was hoping we'd be able to continue our conversation. Tell me what's upsetting you.'

'I'm worried about my future prospects. I know I'm being selfish, but it means a lot to me to be working with this firm, and now I'm not sure where I fit in.'

Michael gave a half smile.

'There are going to be some changes and some big challenges. I hope you are ready to share them with me.'

A New Start

'First of all, what exactly is it you're worried about?' Michael pushed his hair out of his eyes.

'You said there'd be more work.'

'I also said I am aware there's a limit to what anyone can do.'

'I know. If you'll just let me finish . . . '

Michael put a finger to his lips and smiled as she continued.

'The thing is, I'm your secretary, but your father's secretary will take my place, obviously. She's far more experienced and better at the job.'

'And much less fun and funny. And much less pretty!'

Kay could feel the colour rising up her cheeks.

'But she's also moving to Australia. She and her sister have decided they want to make a new start with the assisted passage programme. She hasn't said anything in the office, because she wasn't sure it would all go through. So there isn't a problem.'

He smiled.

'I'd like you to remain as my secretary and help me keep things on track. I'm sure with your support I can ensure Harris and Son, soon to be Harris and Partners, remains the most reputable and flourishing solicitors in the county. It's not going to be easy, I can assure you.'

'You can't imagine how relieved I am, thank you! I know it won't be easy without your dad here, but everything runs pretty smoothly and we have some big clients. They'll all stick with you so long as we carry on doing a good job.'

She rose to leave.

'Just a moment, Kay. I need to tell you something.'

Kay slowly sat down again. Her mind was racing. She told herself not to be ridiculous and imagine he was going to tell her he liked her, or wanted to go out with her on a date.

'Are you listening, Kay?'

'Sorry.'

'I could see your mind was wandering, very unlike you. I'm about to tell you something that I don't want anyone else to know just yet. I think it would dent morale, just at a time when we need to be positive and forward-looking. I received a rather odd letter this morning from Reacher and Good, our biggest client. They are moving their business elsewhere. I couldn't make sense of what was said at all. It was as though they knew something I didn't.'

'Why?'

Kay felt indignant. After all the effort they'd put into looking after their legal affairs.

'They say that something has come to light which means they can no longer trust us. I'm going to telephone them today and see if we can arrange an appointment to get to the bottom of this. I'd like you to come with me.

Meanwhile, not a word to anyone, please.'

'Of course not. I'm very sorry, Michael, and just at the time when your father's leaving, and you're trying to make a go of things.'

'I couldn't have put it better myself.' Michael grimaced. 'Now, I think we'd better get on with the work we do have!'

Back at her desk Kay found it difficult to concentrate. She decided to go to the stock cupboard and see how Betty was getting on with the task of stocktaking.

It was a job she liked doing herself, but had thought she should delegate now that she was the boss's secretary and had more important things to do. It was also helping Betty learn new office skills.

'How's it going, Betty?'

'I can't make things add up.' Betty frowned at the clipboard she was holding. 'I know I haven't done this before, but it seems pretty straightforward. So why is some of the stationery missing?'

'I'm sure it'll be a simple mistake. Let's go through it together.'

It was just what she needed to take her mind from what Michael had just told her.

'Some of the headed notepaper is missing, also a box of carbon paper and some typewriter ribbons. Oh, and a stapler.'

'Well, we can get the steps and make sure there's nothing on those top shelves, and go through it all item by item.'

Exhausted and dusty the two young women slumped on the floor.

'We've checked everything. Those items are definitely missing,' Kay said.

'What do we do now?'

'We'll have to tell Mr Michael. That's all he needs!'

'I suppose he has got a lot on his plate, what with his dad retiring.' Betty paused. 'He's quite attractive, isn't he, but he's nearly old enough to be my father. He'd be all right for you, though, Kay!'

* * *

Kay was perplexed by Michael's reaction to the news of the missing stationery. She thought he'd have been angry and surprised, but he showed no sign of being either.

However, she'd picked up on the tenseness of his facial muscles once again. He was probably a bit anxious that things should be perfect so his father could retire with no worries about the business.

He just thanked Kay for letting him know, and she felt she'd been dismissed rather hurriedly.

The door to Michael's office remained firmly shut through the rest of the morning. When everyone returned from their lunch break, Michael was standing by Kay's desk.

'There's to be another meeting in my office on Monday after I've finalised a few things over the weekend,' he said. 'There are some important changes you all need to know about.'

'Can I help at all? You know I won't say anything to the others.'

'I do know you are trustworthy, but I'm afraid you'll have to be patient to find out what's going to happen next.'

When the office staff had assembled once again in Michael's office, he spoke.

'I won't beat about the bush. As you now know, Mr Harris senior is retiring next month. I am very pleased to report that we are opening a bigger office in Blayton soon, as I'm taking on a couple of new solicitors. I've found the right premises and am having it fitted out and decorated. As soon as it's ready we'll open. I estimate a couple of weeks.'

There was a gasp from the staff.

'This means that I will be leaving this office to oversee things there, and I would like to give you the opportunity of coming with me to help. It won't be easy starting from scratch, in a place where we're not known, but I am confident it won't take long to build up a good relationship with the locals and make it a going concern.'

'I can't come, I'm sorry,' Betty said, putting up her hand up to comment. 'I've got my mum to consider.'

Michael smiled at her.

'I quite understand, Betty and I'm sure Mr Harris senior will be pleased to have you here with him while he ties up the loose ends before he retires. Of course, all of you will be given good references should you decide not to join me in Blayton.'

Kay was stunned. Would the move to Blayton be practical for her?

She was surprised Michael had been so secretive and hadn't told her about the transfer. What else had he kept from her?

'Now you know where and when the move will take place, I'd like you all to think about whether you might like to join me. During the coming week, I'll see you all in turn and we'll have a chat about the possibilities.'

Without a doubt Kay knew she

wanted to be with Michael. Her office skills were good, and he'd said he'd like her as his secretary.

It would be a new beginning.

* * *

Although Kay desperately wanted to go to Blayton, she knew that she would have to tell her parents about it. She would be twenty-one shortly, but she liked to have their approval.

She let herself in. Her mother worked so hard, thought Kay as she looked at the still-damp washing hanging around the kitchen. She knew her mother would have been doing the household chores continually throughout the day as well as visiting their elderly neighbour and taking her a dish of dinner.

'I'll lay the table,' she offered after giving her mother a hug and a kiss.

'Busy day, love?' Mr Watson looked over his spectacles at Kay as they sat at table.

She tucked into the cold meat and

bubble and squeak made using the leftovers from the weekend.

'As usual, but Michael told us some more news. The office is moving to Blayton. It's good for business, but not everyone wants to go. Some of us will stay behind to help Mr Harris Senior tie things up here.'

'It's nice to hear they're successful,' her father replied. 'They've a good reputation in town.'

'My goodness, that's a bit tricky for some people, I suppose,' her mother said.

'Yes, I suppose it is.'

Kay knew that living away from home would be more expensive and she wasn't sure she would be able to afford to rent a room, even with the bonus they had been promised in this week's pay packet.

But she desperately wanted to go. She put her knife and fork together and took her plate to the sink.

Standing there she tried to stop the tears from coursing down her cheeks.

Her mother was soon beside her wrapping her arms round her daughter.

'Come on, love. You have to be realistic. Let's do some sums and find out how much rooms in Blayton cost. Your father and I aren't going to stop you if there's any way you can go. We know how much this means to you.'

'Thanks, Mum. I do really want to go, but Michael would give me a good reference if I have to find another job, I'm sure.'

'It may not come to that.'

Once settled at the table again Mrs Watson got busy.

'Now, what about this one?' she said as she circled an advert in the paper with her pencil, then continued to read down the column.

'It doesn't sound promising so far.' Mr Watson tamped tobacco into his pipe a short while later.

'No, quite a few are shared rooms, one has outside facilities and a couple are in the worst areas of the town. There's just one which sounds all right.

29

It's not too expensive. You might be able to manage it. Just. But there'll be no new clothes or nights out with your friends.'

Kay's heart sank as she thought of her future life stuck in a dreary room, sharing a bathroom with strangers and eating horrible meals cooked by an unkempt landlady with no money to treat herself.

On the positive side, she would still be working with Michael and doing a job she loved . . .

She reached for the paper and turned to the job adverts. But there was nothing which appealed, so she cleared the table and washed up the dishes before making an excuse and going to bed.

Again, she couldn't sleep and lay awake thinking about a nice little room in Blayton and the opportunity to venture into the wide world a little.

★　★　★

Kay was unhappy about going to work the next morning hoping, for once, that she wouldn't be summoned to Michael's office. She didn't want to explain to him why she wouldn't be able to transfer to Blayton.

'We've a busy day ahead, Kay,' Michael said as he bounded in, rain dripping from his mackintosh. 'There are all sorts of things we need to finalise regarding the move, and we still haven't set up that meeting with Reacher and Good to find out what the problem is. They seem reluctant to see me. Are you ready? I want to dictate some letters.'

'Yes, of course.' Kay picked up her notebook and pencil and followed him into the office.

'So, why are you looking so unhappy? Let's get that sorted before we start.'

'I made a decision last night. I can't move to Blayton with you.' The words tumbled out.

Michael's face fell.

'I'm deeply disappointed.'

'Of course I'll stay for the move, and then help Mr Harris, but I'd be grateful for a reference.'

'I was relying on you coming. How will I manage without you?'

Michael moved closer to Kay and took her hand. The feel of his flesh on hers caused her heart to patter and for a moment she was distracted.

'There are plenty of good secretaries,' she managed.

'But no-one like you, Kay. We get on so well. I think we have a very special relationship.'

'I agree we work well together. I'm sorry. I talked it over with my parents last night, and there is no way I can leave home.'

'Of course I understand that you must abide by your parents wishes. I don't suppose it would help if I talked to them?'

'No. My mind's made up.' She moved away and settled, poised to work.

Having dictated several letters, Michael

then leaned back in his chair.

'We need to sort out the pay rises.'

'Pay rises?'

'We're going to be expanding, and with more business we'll be busier than ever. I think everyone should benefit from that.'

A frown crossed his face.

'That's if everything goes as I hope. This business with Reacher and Good has rather dented my confidence. But Father says it will be something and nothing, so I'm to carry on with my plans. He has a surprising amount of faith in my abilities!'

'I'm sure he's right. Since I've been working for you all your clients have been very satisfied with your work.'

'Hmm, which is why this business with Reacher and Good is so puzzling. Or maybe not. I might know what's at the bottom of this.'

'Are you going to tell me, or is this another secret?'

'Oh, you're referring to the move. I'm sorry I couldn't tell you about it. I needed to be sure I'd signed the lease on the premises before I said anything — I didn't want people thinking they were moving then being told they couldn't. It's a shame you're not coming with me, Kay.'

Once again Michael took her hand and she was mesmerised by those blue eyes.

'I'm sorry.'

'Please convince your parents, Kay. It's a wonderful opportunity for you, and there's so much going on in Blayton.'

Kay wondered just how large the pay rise might be, and whether it would after all enable her to make the move to the county town.

'I'll talk to them again this evening. They aren't against me going, but they do have a few worries about me moving there. So do I.'

'Tell them I'll make sure you're all right. I promise.'

* * *

'Will you water the beans now, love? That shower we had this morning wasn't enough to soak through to the roots,' her dad called.

Kay refilled the watering can at the water butt.

'I love these warm evenings. Listen to those birds, Dad. Don't they sound happy!'

'They do, but what about you? Are you happy?'

'I did want to go to Blayton. It's a wonderful opportunity to move to a large town and be the boss's secretary.'

'And you're still so young. I always said you're as bright as a button. Still, there'll be other jobs and we like having you here. We'd have missed you if you'd gone.'

Kay sat down and patted the bench beside her.

'Come and sit down, Dad. Michael really wants me to go and he told me today he's giving us all a pay rise. I think I could manage quite comfortably. I'd like to go, but only with the blessing of both of you.'

He nodded.

'I'll go and talk to your mother now, whilst you finish the watering.'

Ten minutes later she entered the kitchen.

'So, what's the verdict?'

'It isn't quite as straightforward as that. We're also a bit worried about you working so closely with Michael. You seem very fond of him and we don't want you to get hurt again.'

Mrs Watson took her daughter's hand.

'I do like him, he's an excellent boss, but I also know that he wouldn't give me a second glance, Mum. He's out of my league, I told you. Besides, what's that saying? Once bitten, twice shy?'

'So you can deal with your feelings?' Her mother looked anxious.

'Of course I can. I like him, that's all.'

Kay didn't want to lie to her parents, but she wasn't quite sure what her feelings for Michael were. All she knew was that she wanted to carry on working for him.

'In that case, your father and I think it will be a wonderful new start for you . . . after what happened.'

A Dinner Date

'What a perfect end to an eventful week,' Michael said when Kay told him the news she would be moving to Blayton after all. He bent his head towards her and planted a kiss on her cheek. 'I'm not going to apologise. Kay, you have no idea how much this means to me.'

Kay didn't know what to say so she kept quiet, but returned Michael's smile.

'I think we should celebrate,' he continued. 'Will you have dinner with me tonight?'

With shining eyes, Kay nodded.

'I'll pick you up at seven-thirty, then.'

The day seemed interminably long to Kay, even though she was in and out of Michael's office taking dictation, on the telephone answering calls from clients and showing Betty how to work the duplicating machine.

'Thanks, Kay,' Betty said. 'I expect you'll be going to Blayton with Mr Michael, won't you?'

'Yes, I will,' Kay replied, trying to keep the excitement out of her voice. 'I'm sure you'll have no difficulty in getting a new job locally once this office closes. Everyone here likes you, and you pick things up quickly.'

'Because you're patient with me. I'll miss you, Kay.'

⋆ ⋆ ⋆

On the dot of seven-thirty that evening Mrs Watson checked her hair in the hall mirror before answering the door to Michael.

'Good evening. How nice to see you again. Do come in.'

Kay appeared in the hallway with her jacket on, ready to go, but Michael seemed to be in no rush to leave. He followed Mrs Watson through to the sitting room and shook hands with Mr Watson.

'I know Kay will be in safe hands with you, Michael,' her father was saying, 'but she's still our daughter and I'd like you to get her home in good time this evening.'

Kay could feel her stomach contracting as she listened to her father issuing orders to her boss!

'I was planning on driving to Blayton for our meal, sir,' Michael replied, not looking put out in the least. 'I can't promise what time we'll be back, but I can assure you I will look after Kay.'

It was wonderful to be beside Michael in his very modern Austin sports car. The evening was a little chilly, but Kay had agreed that it would be fun to drive with the top down and had tied a scarf around her hair so that she didn't look like a wreck when they arrived at the restaurant.

'I like your car. It's a lovely colour,' Kay said touching the paintwork on the inside of the door.

'The colour's speedwell blue,' Michael said, turning briefly to look at her.

She couldn't help comparing the colour of the car with his eyes which were a much stronger colour, deeper and more intense.

'We don't have a car, but we've borrowed one from a friend a few times to go on holiday. Dad can drive, but I think he prefers his bike.'

'It's a bit of an indulgence having a car like this, but it's fun, don't you think?'

'I love it.'

From time to time Michael took one hand from the steering wheel and lightly touched Kay's hand.

'We could go dancing after we've eaten, if you like,' he shouted over the engine noise.

Kay stiffened and withdrew her hand from his. He pulled the car over to the side of the road and stopped.

'What is it? What did I say wrong?'

Kay took a deep breath.

'I had an understanding with a man I used to dance with. We were quite good, in fact, and won several competitions. I

41

don't like to mention things like that at work because it's not appropriate. Anyway, I thought George and I had a future together, but he waltzed off with someone else he met at a competition, and didn't even have the courage to tell me to my face. Just posted a letter to me.'

Even after all these months, Kay could feel the humiliation she'd felt at the time. She looked across at Michael and realised that perhaps George had done her a favour. After all, if it hadn't been for him, she wouldn't be here with Michael now.

'That's in the past,' she said firmly. 'I've a lot to look forward to.'

Michael took her hand and raised it to his lips.

'So have I, Kay. I feel privileged to be in your company.'

He started the engine and they sped off again towards Blayton.

Kay was glad she'd protected her hair from being blown about, as the restaurant was very stylish. She accepted a small sherry and the waiter handed her the menu. It had never been her habit to dine out so she felt a bit at sea.

It was as if Michael sensed this as he leaned over.

'I'm having prawn cocktail, steak and a lovely messy pudding. How about you?'

'That sounds delicious. I'll have the same.'

With the order given, Kay sipped her sherry. She glanced towards the window and blinked hard.

'Isn't that Charlie over there? Fancy him being here. Doesn't he look smart! I never understood why he left in such a hurry. Should we go over, do you think?'

'No!' Michael said sharply. Then he softened his tone. 'I don't want to share you, Kay. That's one reason I brought you out here — so that we wouldn't see anyone we knew.'

'You're not ashamed of me, are you?'

'Quite the contrary.' He picked up his glass and held it in a toast to her. 'To the best companion anyone could wish to have.'

'That was tasty,' Kay said, having finished the last scrap of her prawn cocktail.

'Good, you looked as though you were enjoying it. Apart from enjoying eating out what else do you like to do?'

'We have fish and chips once a week from the chip shop, but it is lovely being waited on in a restaurant.'

'One of the things I like about you, Kay, is you don't put on any airs and graces. You're comfortable being you. Some of the women at the tennis club pretend they're something they're not. I don't like it. But you still haven't told me about your hobbies.'

'I like going to the pictures. As I said, I used to dance. I started when I was quite little. Mum and Dad managed to pay for classes and I got quite good. And then . . . '

'George?'

'Yes. I needed a partner so my dance teacher introduced me to George. We got on really well and he was a good dancer. I have trophies from when we were together. Well, you know the rest.'

'But why have you stopped dancing, just because George left? Surely there are other men who could be your partner!'

'I don't know. I gave up. It was an awful time.'

It seemed strange that she was telling him all about her break up with George. She hadn't talked much about it at the time, even though she'd been devastated. It felt good getting it off her chest to Michael.

'I'd quite like to learn to dance.' He smiled. 'I have had to dance at functions, but I'm pretty useless. I usually end up treading on my partner's shoes.'

'Maybe — no, that's a silly idea.'

'Go on.'

'I was going to say, maybe I could teach you.'

'I'd like that very much. Once the move is over and we're less busy, let's do it.'

Their conversation was interrupted by the waiter bringing the steaks. Michael poured them each a glass of red wine. Kay remembered that Charlie was in the restaurant, but when she looked over he'd disappeared.

Through the rest of the meal, Michael enthused about the new office, the town and the plans he had for the company when he would be in charge. Kay watched as his face lit up as he talked.

'I'm so pleased things are working well for you,' she said.

'And what about you? Are you feeling happier now you can see your future changing?'

'The main difficulty will be finding somewhere to live,' Kay confessed. 'I'm used to being at home and I like my creature comforts. I wouldn't like to share facilities and anything else would be much more expensive, although the pay rise is welcome.'

'I could help if you'd let me,' Michael invited.

'In what way?'

'Putting out enquiries, making a few calls to contacts, that sort of thing.'

'That wouldn't be fair on the others, would it? I don't want any sort of favouritism.'

'No use offering you a loan of money, then?'

'Certainly not!' Kay was appalled. That wasn't what she wanted at all.

'I didn't mean to offend you. Let's change the subject. I'll tell you about the tennis club. You might consider joining the one in Blayton. I'm a member there. I could introduce you to a few people.'

Kay thought she might be out of her depth there after what he'd said about some of the women, but he was so excited about her joining she didn't like to dent his enthusiasm.

'There are some nice people there too, as well as those tiresome women. And I need a partner, Kay. I'm always being asked to play doubles.'

'I'm not sure.' The only time Kay had

played tennis was at school. 'I've never been good at sport.'

'Let's agree. I'll teach you to play tennis and you'll teach me to dance. What do you say?'

'I say we each have quite a challenge!'

The meal ended after a creamy dessert, and coffee in small cups. Michael signalled for the bill and helped Kay on with her jacket. As they passed the place where Kay had seen Charlie, she paused.

'It was rude of us not to speak to Charlie.'

His face grim, Michael didn't respond as he held the door open for her.

Back in the car Kay laid a hand on Michael's arm. There was something bothering him and she felt as though she'd spoiled the evening by mentioning Charlie again. If only she'd kept her mouth shut.

'I just want to say I've had a marvellous evening. Thank you.'

'It was my pleasure, the most

enjoyable evening I've had in a long time. Thank you.' He paused. 'I hope we can do it again some time soon.'

Kay's heart gave a little skip, then she remembered the promise she'd made herself after receiving George's letter. To try to let her head rule her heart.

'Maybe.'

Michael sat quiet for a moment more.

'I'm sorry about back there in the restaurant. It's just that there's something you don't know about Charlie.' He did not elaborate, and Kay didn't liked to force the issue. Neither of them spoke on the drive home.

She wasn't surprised to see the lights on downstairs. She knew her parents would be waiting up to make sure she got home safely.

'Here we are.' Michael leaped out of the car and held the door open before walking her to the front door. 'Thank you again.'

He leaned forward as if he were going to kiss her, but appeared to think better of it and gave her shoulder a quick pat.

'Good night, Kay.'

'Night, Michael. I'll see you on Monday.'

The front door opened as Michael made his way back down the path. He turned and gave her a wave.

'Nice evening, love?' her mum asked.

'Lovely. It was really posh. We had prawn cocktail and steak.'

'Come on into the kitchen. Your dad's just made some hot chocolate. You need bringing back down to earth!' Her mum chuckled. 'You should hear her, Harry, with her prawn cocktails and steaks.'

'I'm ever so tired, Mum. I think I'll head upstairs. I'm going to take the bus to Blayton tomorrow and have a look for somewhere to live.'

* * *

Kay had cut sandwiches for her lunch and packed a bag with a notebook and pencil. She intended finding a place to live before she returned home later in the afternoon.

Of course, Blayton wasn't that far away, but her father had been right when he'd pointed out that the travelling time and expense would not be viable. In a way she was excited at the prospect of being independent of her parents, but she was also a bit apprehensive.

Walking along the High Street, she passed a couple of estate agents and looked in their windows. There were a few advertisements which looked promising and she went in and told them what she required.

'If you want something self-contained,' the first agent said, sucking his teeth, 'you'll not find it cheaply.' He named a figure which made Kay sit up. There was no way she could afford that sort of money on a weekly basis, with or without a pay rise.

The second agent said much the same thing, adding helpfully, 'If you go along towards the park you might see a board outside a house saying there's accommodation to let.'

Feeling hopeful once more Kay set off, glancing down the side streets in search of an elusive notice. Her eyes widened in delight as she saw a very different notice in front of her. On a hoarding outside a brand-new office block there was written in large fancy script: *Harris & Partners, Solicitors.* So this was where the new office would be! It was very central and a lot of the Saturday shoppers were taking an interest.

Peering in through the window, she was delighted and surprised to see Michael inside. Fearing he would catch her prying, she edged away, then a window opened.

'Kay! What are you doing here? Have you come to help me with the decorating?'

Kay had never seen him dressed like this, wearing an old sweater with a hole in the sleeve. It looked as if he hadn't shaved that morning, and in one hand he held a brush which was dripping pale cream paint down his front.

She laughed up at him.

'I'm flat-hunting. I don't mind helping you later on, but I'm not really dressed for it.'

'I'll let you carry on your important search. Let me know how you get on.'

A couple of turnings along, there was the notice Kay was looking for. It must be fate, she decided, striding up to the front door and banging on it.

The room she was shown into was appalling; it was dirty and smelt of cabbage. She was told there was a bathroom upstairs she could share with three of the other tenants, and a kettle and mini oven was provided in the room. Kay couldn't possibly see herself living there and made her exit as quickly as possible, the smell still clinging to her nostrils.

Determined not to be put off, and with the thought of Michael wanting to know how she got on, she renewed her search.

After two more unsuccessful attempts, she was on the verge of giving up. She decided to sit in the park and take stock. It was a beautiful park with children playing and the birds were singing, as if willing her to be positive.

Taking a different gate which she hoped would get her back to the High Street, Kay spotted another notice advertising accommodation. She might as well give it a go, there was nothing to lose.

'Come in and see for yourself,' the woman who answered her knock invited. 'We'll go upstairs first and I'll show you the bedroom that's to let.'

The house was clean and smelled of furniture polish. Kay dared not get her hopes up too much. The room she was shown into was a large one at the back of the house. It overlooked an unkempt garden.

The room itself was simply furnished with a single bed along one wall covered with a colourful patchwork quilt. The wardrobe was large and more than adequate to hold Kay's clothes. A comfortable chair and a dressing-table with stool completed the furnishings.

Everything looked so cosy Kay felt she could be very happy here. There was even a tiny wash basin tucked away in a small cupboard. The curtains were a buttercup yellow and the carpet on the floor was emblazoned with flowers.

'The bathroom's next door, and you'd be free to have as many baths as you wished,' the woman aid. 'I don't charge extra for heating and lighting. The rent is all-inclusive; you'll find no hungry meters here!' She laughed as she spoke. 'I sleep at the front of the house, just along the landing. You'd only be sharing with me.'

They went downstairs again and into a cosy kitchen.

'Do you enjoy cooking?'

Kay thought about it.

'I'm not very good. Mum takes care

of the household chores. I help Dad in the garden.'

'There's a garden, too. I'm not very clever with that side of things, but it's nice to potter in the sunshine when it's out. Come and have a look in the sitting-room.'

After her tour of the comfortable house with this very pleasant woman, Kay felt there must be a catch and it would probably be the rent.

'How much are you asking?' she said, crossing her fingers that she'd be in luck and able to afford it.

The amount quoted was very reasonable.

'I don't charge a lot, but I'm particular who I agree to let to. I like you, and if you can see yourself living here with me, please take as long as you need to decide.'

'I'd like the room, please!' she blurted out, sure she was doing the right thing.

The woman nodded.

'My name's Olive,' she said holding out her hand.

'And I'm Kay, Kay Watson. I'm going to be working for the solicitors in the High Street.'

'Oh, I see.' Olive wore a guarded look.

'Harris and Partners,' Kay added, hoping to give the firm a bit of publicity.

Olive beamed.

'The new ones? I thought you might have meant Twigge and Moore.'

'I work for Michael Harris at the moment and will be moving here when the new office opens.'

'I'll have to take up references,' Olive told her. 'Give me your details and I'll let you know when I've heard back.'

When Kay left Elm Close she felt like skipping along the road and singing. Her feet instinctively took her back to Michael's new office where she knocked at the door.

He looked out of the window and beckoned her inside.

'You look happy.' He put down his paintbrush and placed his hands on her shoulders. 'Any luck?'

57

'The best. I've found somewhere to live!' Kay delved into her bag and brought out her packet of sandwiches. 'Not quite as posh as last night, but would you like to share my lunch? Ham or cheese?'

★   ★   ★

'Mmm, these are good.' Michael took another bite.

'Glad you like them. If you've got a knife I'll cut the apple in half.'

'All mod cons here, you know. I'll fetch a knife and put the kettle on when I've finished this.'

As they sat with their mugs of tea Kay told him all about Olive and the room.

'She would like a reference, if you wouldn't mind.'

'Of course. What do you think of my decorating?'

'It's very good, very tasteful. I'm quite happy to give you a hand this afternoon. My search didn't take as long as I expected. I feel so lucky!'

'Me, too,' Michael mumbled, half to himself. 'I've an old shirt in a bag somewhere that I was using for decorating last time I was here. Would that do?'

'Lovely, thanks. Oh, I forgot to tell you Olive mentioned our rivals here, Twigge and Moore. She didn't seem too impressed with them.'

'I think they're having a spot of bother. They had a good name, but are so busy I imagine it's very hard for Mr Twigge to keep an eye on everything. They've expanded and taken on new staff, and there have been a few rumours going round the town. Nothing for us to worry about.' But there was the same tenseness in his face Kay had seen when they'd been talking about Charlie.

Michael quickly disappeared into another room and returned clutching a paint-stained shirt.

'Here we are, try this for size. I'll get you a pot of paint and brush.'

Kay enjoyed the afternoon with Michael. Some of the time they worked in silence, and some of the time they chatted. She was happy they were friends, but she also felt a strange intimacy wearing an item of his clothing. The shirt smelt of Michael, distinctively masculine.

Standing back to admire her work, she felt satisfied.

'I think it's time I was getting back. I'll leave you to clean the brushes.' She handed him her brush and paint pot, then took off the shirt and gave that to him, too.

'Hold on.' Michael searched in his pocket for a hankie. 'You can't go on the bus with paint on your face.'

He wiped her cheek then gently caressed her face with his fingers. She didn't want to stop him, but she remembered her mum saying she didn't want her to be hurt again.

'I've got to go or I'll miss my bus.'

'What bus? They run every half an hour. Does it matter which one you catch? Let's go out again.'

Kay burst out laughing.

'I'm not going out with you looking like that!'

Michael looked down at himself.

'No, you're probably right. Maybe another time?'

'Maybe. See you Monday.'

As Kay left the office she was aware of someone peering down the side alley.

'Charlie! You gave me a fright.'

'Kay, lovely to see you. How's tricks?'

'Good. The move is going really well. It's such a shame you left when you did.'

'Not really, Kay. I'm not sure I should tell you this, with you being a secretary in the firm. Are you catching the bus back? Let me walk with you and I'll tell you something which might be to your advantage.'

Charlie was looking very smart in some expensive-looking new clothes.

'You're doing all right for yourself, Charlie!'

'Better than all right. I work for

Twigge and Moore. They're a much bigger firm so there are a lot of opportunities for anyone with a bit of ambition. I'm doing well there. Mr Harris was sorry when I left. Gave me an excellent reference, of course. Practically begged me to reconsider. No chance.'

'I'm glad you're doing OK, but sorry you didn't tell us you were leaving. You should have had a bit of a do.'

'It's all right. Mr Twigge wanted me to start with them straight away, so I decided not to tell the others.'

Kay tripped on an uneven pavement and Charlie caught her arm.

'Here,' he said tucking her arm through his, 'I'll make sure you don't fall.'

Kay felt uncomfortable as she had never really taken to Charlie. She'd been aware that some of his comments at work were inappropriate and not long before he'd left she'd found Betty in tears after he'd said something to her.

They'd kept it to themselves not wanting to make a fuss, but Kay had said if it happened again Betty was to tell her and they'd report Charlie to Mr Michael.

'What was it you wanted to tell me?'

'I'm not sure I should.'

'You said you would.'

'Well, Reacher and Good have taken their business away from Harris and Son because they learned of some dubious things going on.'

'What sort of things?'

'That would be telling. Here we are, Kay.' He patted her hand before releasing her. 'If you decide you want to work for Twigge and Moore I'll put in a good word for you. And for anyone else who wants to join. Spread the word.'

He winked at her before disappearing into the crowd of shoppers returning home.

A Dance Lesson

'Are those letters ready for signing yet, Kay?' Michael called her attention.

'Sorry, Michael, I haven't finished them. I'll work through and get them done.'

'No need for that. Actually I was hoping you'd join me in my office. I've got some cheese and pickle sandwiches, a scotch egg and a couple of cold sausages.'

Michael was sitting waiting, the food spread out on his desk.

'I'm sorry about the letters.'

'It's not like you. You've been very quiet and thoughtful this morning. I hope you aren't having second thoughts about coming to work for me in Blayton.'

'No, not at all. It's something else I feel uneasy about, but I don't like to mention it because I think I might upset you.'

'Oh, Kay, it takes a lot to upset me.'

'But I'm pretty sure this will. I wasn't going to say anything, but I met Charlie after I left you on Saturday. He was lurking outside your new offices and told me all about how he'd left us for his new job at Twigge and Moore. And how much you wanted to keep him.'

'That's not true!' Michael burst out. He opened his mouth as if to say more, but then seemed to change his mind.

'I expect I'm being silly, but has this anything at all to do with Reacher and Good?'

'What makes you think that?'

'You have the same expression whenever they or Charlie are mentioned. Can't you tell me what's going on, Michael? I am connected to the firm, after all, and we are friends, aren't we?'

Michael took the cup from Kay and put it on the desk. Holding her hand he assured her that they were indeed friends.

'If you don't mind, Kay, I'd like to

keep things a bit close to my chest for a little longer, as I'm not sure of the facts. Dad has heard from Tom Reacher and he wants to go over things with me.'

Kay left Michael's office and returned to her desk, determined to erase everything else from her mind, at least until she'd got her work up to date. She used to be efficient and she didn't want to blot her copybook before she'd even got to be the boss's secretary.

* * *

At home, after the evening meal, Kay went up to her room to sort through her belongings. She wanted time to herself. It was going to be such an adventure to be living on her own in Blayton.

Her parents had been quietly happy when she'd described Olive and her nice house to them. Of course, her mother wanted to make sure they were both as good as she said, but Kay decided that when she went to Blayton she would go on her own. However, having looked at the things she'd amassed on her bedroom floor to take with her, she knew the trunk would have to be brought down from the attic and she'd need help transferring everything.

Her thoughts wandered to the new office she'd be working in and she realised that, although she'd painted a wall, she hadn't toured the premises and was none the wiser as to what it contained. She had no idea who else would be going to Blayton and she hoped she wouldn't be running into Charlie too often.

Michael was absent from the office for the next couple of days. Kay knew he was busy with clients who preferred a home visit from him. He had a nice way with him and accommodated people as much as he could whilst still remaining in charge.

By Thursday he was back in the office.

Betty pounced immediately she saw him.

'Tea, Mr Michael?'

He looked surprised.

'I'll wait until everyone else has theirs, thanks, Betty,' he said, going through to his office.

'Only, I wanted a word,' she pressed.

Kay looked up, wondering what was going on.

'Come on in.' Michael held the door open for Betty.

When they emerged a good ten minutes later Betty's face was pink and her eyes moist. Kay took her to the kitchen area where they could be private.

'Whatever's upset you?'

'Mum said I was to ask if I could leave at once, and not wait for Mr Harris to retire. She said I could go and work in the bakery because there's a vacancy there now. I don't want to, but she said I had to do what I was told.'

'Why doesn't your mum want you to stay here?' Kay did not understand why Betty should give up her job particularly when she was doing so well.

'I told her about Mr Harris retiring and Mr Michael moving, and she said where did that leave me? She said I'd be better off out of it and if that was all the thanks I got from Harris and Son I shouldn't give them the time of day.'

Deciding not to wade through the whole story, Kay said, 'You are learning new skills here, and your work is highly thought of by all of us. What did Mr Michael say?'

Betty shrugged her shoulders.

'He said it was up to me, but he did offer to talk to Mum.'

Kay wondered how many employers would be bothered to do that. Perhaps she could help.

'I'll have a word with Mr Michael, shall I?'

'I'm sorry, Kay. I'm being a nuisance.'

She knocked on Michael's door.

'It's such a shame Betty's mother wants her to work in the bakery. All she'd be doing is the cleaning, mopping floors and things like that. She's doing so well here.'

Michael looked worried.

'I'm very sorry for her, and I do understand her mother's wish to keep her in employment. I'd like to go and see her and explain the situation. I suppose there's no way she could move to the new office.'

'Hardly, even with the pay rise she wouldn't be able to afford anything except something shabby. Let me talk to her mother. I'll tell her Betty will get a very good reference from you, and that she has a good future ahead.'

'Would you, Kay? I'm sure it will be better if you go — a woman's touch.'

'I'll go in my lunch hour.'

Kay was very happy with the way her meeting with Betty's mother went. She wasn't an ogre, just trying to do the best for her daughter. Kay had even suggested that when she was settled in

Blayton Betty might visit her. Permission had been granted as Betty's mother had deemed Kay to be a sensible young woman.

After Kay had finished telling Michael about her visit to Betty's home, he leaned back in his chair and grinned.

'Quite the diplomat, aren't you? Is there no end to your skills?'

Kay smiled back.

'I'm glad I could help.'

'I've been busy too. I made a few calls, and one of my acquaintances at the tennis club has a vacancy for a junior at his office just down the road. He will be very happy to take Betty on after she's finished here. He'd like to interview her, of course, but I'm sure Betty will charm him.'

'Now that we've got Betty sorted out, I've a bit of good news for you, Kay,' Michael said the next day.

She raised her eyebrows and he gestured for her to sit down.

'I've had a telephone call from a Miss Olive Carter.'

Kay couldn't remember a client with that name, and then it came to her.

'You mean my landlady? Well, hopefully she will be.'

'The same. I gave you a glowing reference and she said she's happy to let you have the room and you can move in as soon as you like.'

'That's wonderful! All I'll need to do then is take my stuff over somehow.' Kay didn't know how she'd manage to get all her things moved.

'I can help with that. My car's not much use for transporting luggage, but Dad will lend me his.'

'I'm sure I'll manage.'

'It's all right, Kay, I'd like to help you. Now, about this evening.'

'This evening? What about it?'

'You promised to teach me to dance and I thought, if you're free tonight, I could have my first lesson. How about going to the Orchid Ballroom in Blayton?'

★   ★   ★

72

Kay sighed as she surveyed the pile of discarded clothes on her bed. She checked her watch. She had just fifteen minutes before Michael arrived.

'Can I come in, love?' Her mum walked in and sat on the edge of the bed. 'I thought you might be having trouble finding something to wear. I wonder if this might do. I bought it for you as a present for when you left, but maybe you'd like it now.' She held up a bright cotton floral dress in green and pinks. Kay fingered the ric rac trim and admired the oversize buttons on the shoulders.

'It's lovely, Mum, thank you!' After giving her mum a tight squeeze, she hurriedly put the dress on before spinning round and enjoying the feel of the fullness of the tiered and ruffled skirt.

She flung open the wardrobe to look at her reflection in the mirror on the inside of the door. A slim young woman with flowing wavy chestnut hair, milk chocolate brown eyes and a pretty smile stared back at her. She fingered the material of the dress and pulled it down over her hips a little bit. Her smile broadened as she turned to her mother. 'What do you think?'

'It fits perfectly. Slip your shoes on and show your dad.'

Kay felt like a princess and couldn't wait for Michael to arrive. As soon as she heard his tap on the front door she rushed to open it. He was dressed in a light tan suit with a conker-coloured shirt. Kay felt a rush of happiness as she contemplated an evening ahead with Michael.

'You look gorgeous, Kay,' Michael said as he looked her up and down.

She felt like bouncing down the path to the car, but walked sedately knowing that it wouldn't be long before she and Michael were dancing to the sound of the big bands. She realised she was quite happily going to the ballroom without George, something she never thought she'd bring herself to do.

Perhaps, at last, she was getting over him.

'Two left feet? You're a much better dancer than you said,' Kay remarked as they twirled around the dance floor.

'It must be because I have such a good partner. Ready for the next one?'

'Goodness, I suppose it's the tennis that keeps you fit. I have to say I'm a bit out of puff as I haven't been doing much recently.'

'Would you like to sit the next one out?'

'No, I want to dance all night long. Ready?'

With the light reflecting from the glitter ball and the music pounding across the hall Kay felt as though she was in heaven. She always felt alive when she was dancing and being with Michael seemed to heighten all her senses. At the end of the next dance they collapsed in each other's arms, laughing.

'May I have the next dance please, Kay?'

George was standing next to her, gripping her elbow.

'Go ahead, I'm getting a drink.' Michael walked off without a backward glance.

'I've been watching you. Your new dance partner isn't quite up to scratch, is he? Won any competitions?' George smirked. 'Let's see if you remember how to dance when you've got a proper partner.' George took her hand in his and held her close.

'Get off me, George!' Kay pulled her hand out of his grasp and shoved him away. She pushed through the crowded dance floor and made her way out to the street to breathe in the cool air. Leaning against the wall she gave a deep sigh of relief. She had never seen George like that before, and from the smell of his breath guessed he'd been drinking.

'Is everything all right, Kay?' Michael was at her side looking concerned. 'I saw you run out. What happened?'

'I didn't want to dance with the man

who asked me, that's all,' Kay said, fighting to stay calm.

'Did he make a nuisance of himself?' Michael narrowed his eyes and looked into the bright lights of the ballroom.

'Not in that way.' Kay sighed. 'That was George. I think he'd probably had a beer too many. He's gone now.'

'Would you like to leave? Shall I fetch your things?'

'No, I'd like a glass of lemon squash and then I'd like to jive, please.'

Michael escorted Kay inside and found her a seat. Her immediate thought was that she'd had a lucky escape from George. Her life had changed for the better in every way. She was completely over him now and that realisation gave her freedom.

The beat of the jive music and the fast movements kept them both literally on their toes as they cavorted on the dance floor. When the music ended a spontaneous round of applause broke out and laughter filled the room.

'I never knew dancing could be such

fun!' Michael said, his lips close to her ear so that she could hear what he was saying. 'The music seems to take over, doesn't it?'

'That's exactly how I feel,' she replied.

When the last waltz struck up, Kay and Michael fitted easily into each other's arms. He led her around the room, one arm high on her back with the other one gently holding her hand. When the last strains receded and the dance was over, Michael bent his head and pressed his cheek against Kay's. She didn't pull away.

Leaving Home

Kay decided not to tell her parents all of the events at the Orchid Ballroom.

'I had a nice time and it was good to be dancing again. Michael's quite good.'

'Will you return to your competition dancing, do you think?'

Kay considered the question.

'No, I'll just dance for pleasure now. I'll have more than enough to occupy me with all the other things going on in Blayton.'

'Remember we're always here for you if you need us.'

Kay felt a rush of warm affection for her parents; they'd always been supportive of her.

'I'll miss your cooking, Mum!'

Mrs Watson looked worried.

'I hope that's not all you'll miss. I'd like to see where you're going to be and meet your landlady, love.'

'It's all right, Mum. Olive is lovely, I'm sure you'll take to her. My room's really nice, too.

'As soon as I'm settled you must come over and see for yourself. You'll feel so much better then. Please don't worry about me, I'm a big girl now.'

Kay reached over and squeezed her mum's hand.

'She'll worry all right, you know your mother,' her dad said comfortingly. 'But I think it'll be good for you to get away from reminders of that George who let you down so badly.'

Kay thought back to that time, remembering how she'd felt when he'd left her.

'I feel better about George now. I suppose it's because I have so much else on my mind.'

She was no longer sure what she'd seen in George, except for the fact that he was good at dancing. She supposed she'd been swept away with all the excitement and glamour of the competitions.

'I expect you'll meet all sorts of new people. They'll be getting a new accounts clerk to replace Charlie. You might get on well with him.'

'Honestly, Mum, one minute you're telling me to be careful in case I get my heart broken again, and then you're trying to matchmake!'

'Well, I like Michael, but he's not suitable, is he?'

Kay decided to change the subject. It didn't matter whether or not Michael was suitable. They were friends, that was all.

'Dad, I'm going to need that old trunk down from the attic to take my things. Would we be able to get it down after lunch? Michael's coming to help me move my stuff at three.'

She noticed her mother raising her eyebrows at her father, but decided not to say anything. Now she would enjoy the treacle sponge and custard they were having for pudding.

Kay had just managed to close the lid of the trunk by sitting on it when she heard voices in the hall.

'My trunk's ready, Dad!' she called.

Michael came bounding up the stairs, closely followed by Mr Watson. The two men carried the heavy trunk down the stairs with care, trying to avoid damaging the paintwork.

Kay picked up a holdall and her handbag and stood for a second, taking a last quick look round her room. Her much-loved, lopsided teddy bear sat on the bed, looking rather forlorn.

'Oh, OK. I was going to leave you behind, but I suppose you'd better come.'

She tucked the bear under her arm and, feeling rather sad that she was leaving the room she'd had all her life, she headed for the stairs and a fresh start.

* * *

'Your parents seem quite happy about you moving.'

'I'm not sure Mum is. She really

wants to see where I'm living, to make sure. It will be strange for them, being on their own again. I'm an only child.'

'I don't have any brothers or sisters, either.' This confirmed what Kay had heard about Michael. She didn't say anything, as he was busy negotiating a series of bends in the road.

'My favourite bit of the journey is just coming up ahead. The woods are beautiful at all times of the year, of course, but now in spring they're superb. Shall we stop and have a quick walk, or would you rather get to your new home and settle in?'

Kay was happy to agree to a walk in the sunshine. She followed Michael carefully along a narrow pathway.

'It's so pretty when the sun shines through the leaves like that.'

'That's not the only pretty thing in these woods.'

Kay held her breath.

'Look at these stunning yellow flowers,' he continued.

She tried not to show her disappointment.

'I wish I knew a bit more about wild flowers and their names. Shall we pick some for Miss Carter? I think she'd like them.'

They both set to work picking the flowers, then Michael cut a bit of foliage with his penknife before they decided they had enough and set off back for the car.

In Elm Close, at Michael's insistence, Kay went ahead to ring the front door bell. She glanced back to the parked car and Michael, who was struggling to unload the heavy trunk single-handedly. Wondering if she should have insisted on helping, the decision was taken out of her hands as Olive Carter opened the front door.

'Kay, how lovely to see you! Come along in.'

Kay handed over the bunch of flowers.

'We picked these on the way. I hope you like them.'

'They are beautiful, thank you.' She peered out at the car.

'That's Michael Harris, my boss. He gave me a lift over here, but the trunk's a bit heavy!' Together they watched Michael heave it from his father's car and manoeuvre it up the front path.

He smiled at Olive as Kay introduced them.

'Leave the luggage in the hallway and Kay can unpack from there. Save chipping my staircase!' She looked at Kay and winked ever so slightly. 'I've just made tea. I'll fetch cups and saucers for you two and pop these flowers in some water. Kay, take Michael into the sitting-room and make yourself at home. I hope you'll be happy here.'

'She seems nice.' Michael flopped down into a fireside chair and looked around the room. 'This place has a comfortable feel to it.'

'That's what I thought. I'm lucky to have found it.'

'So,' Olive said, returning with the

crockery, 'you're the solicitor who's moving into the new premises in the High Street. Was it you I spoke to on the telephone, about Kay?'

'That's right, Miss Carter. I . . . '

She interrupted him.

'You both must call me Olive. Miss Carter makes me feel old.'

Kay watched Olive as she chatted easily to Michael. The woman was older than her mother, probably around sixty, with a fuzz of greyish-white hair in a halo around her plump face.

Her movements were slow and deliberate, and it seemed as if nothing would upset her easily. She was looking forward to finding out a bit more about her landlady. Kay was sure she would have an interesting history.

Suddenly she remembered her handbag, which she'd forgotten to bring in from the car. It was still stuffed behind the front passenger seat. Excusing herself, she went to retrieve it.

'Kay's a very valuable member of our work force,' Michael was telling Olive when she returned to the house. 'I'm glad she's found such a pleasant place to live, and that you'll be taking care of her. You're very welcome to visit our office any time you like.'

'Thank you, Michael, I'll bear that in mind when I need the assistance of a solicitor. It's good to know what's happening in town, though. I think you're one of the first companies to move into the block. There's a lot of change going on.'

After half an hour, Michael made his excuses and left Elm Close.

'Thank you very much for all you've done, Michael,' said Kay seeing him off at the front door.

'Glad to help,' he replied. 'I'll be in the office bright and early tomorrow morning, although I'm not sure what we'll be doing, as everything will still be new.'

He looked a bit forlorn, Kay thought as he walked to his car.

Olive's suggestion of unpacking downstairs and transferring her belongings up to her room had been a good one. Kay looked around the unfamiliar room and felt a bit homesick. Blinking away momentary feelings of sadness, she sat on the bed and fished around for something very important.

'Well, Teddy,' she addressed her bear, 'it's just you and me now. We'll be all right, won't we?'

'I've made a salad, Kay!' Olive said.

'Coming!' She propped Teddy up on her pillow and went downstairs.

Over the meal, Olive said, 'I'll prepare breakfast for you each morning, about eight o'clock, if that's OK. You haven't far to go to work. At the weekends I'll leave you to get your own, because I know you young people sometimes like a lie-in. What do you like to eat?'

'Almost everything. I'm not keen on offal.'

'No stuffed hearts, then?'

'No, thank you!'

'I like making puddings and baking. It was a bit of a job during the war

88

years and after, until rationing finished. I used to swap things I wasn't bothered about for flour, eggs and sugar.'

'I love puddings.'

'My downfall is boiled sweets.' Olive reached into the pocket of her cardigan and pulled out a paper bag. 'Humbugs. We'll have one with our cup of tea. Now, what time do you finish work?'

'Six o'clock.'

'That's what I thought. I'll have a meal for you at about seven. If you're going out to eat perhaps you'd give me as much notice as possible.'

'Not likely. Where would I go?'

'I think your boss, Michael, might ask you out for a meal?' Olive smiled.

Kay felt her cheeks growing warm.

'I have been out with him, to dinner and to the Orchid Ballroom, dancing.'

'Then I'm sure there will be many more occasions.'

'He's a good friend, that's all,' Kay protested, spearing a piece of cucumber and popping it in her mouth.

Kay helped Olive to clear the table

and washed up the few bits of crockery.

'It'll help me find out where things live.' When everything was neat and tidy once again, Kay said, 'Can I look at the garden, please?'

'Of course. I'll come with you.'

Together they toured the straggly area.

'As I said when I first showed you round, I don't do much out here.'

Kay wondered what her dad would have thought. He prided himself on keeping their garden at home neat and tidy. There were always fresh vegetables growing, and a pretty array of flowers which her mum would pick for the vases in the house.

'I don't mind cutting the grass,' she offered, hoping Olive wouldn't take offence.

'Great, I was hoping you'd say that!' Olive let out a giggle which took Kay by surprise. This woman had unexpected qualities. 'Do what you like with it.'

She shivered.

'I'm going in now, it's a bit chilly.'

She pulled her cardigan around her and headed towards the back door.

Kay remained in the garden a little longer. It would be good to have a project which didn't involve work. Or Michael. She didn't want to be in a situation where she became reliant on him, substituting Michael for her parents; she'd soon be twenty-one and she needed to gain independence.

She had another quick walk round the garden and tried to see it through her father's eyes.

He would want to produce as many vegetables and as much salad as possible. She'd draw a diagram and decide how best to use the space.

Olive had seemed very pleased with the flowers, so she would definitely grow flowers to cut — maybe dahlias and chrysanthemums. She was sure Olive would be pleased if there was fresh produce to eat, as well.

The evening was growing dark and it was time to go back inside the house. There was a television in the corner of the sitting-room, but Olive had the radio tuned to a music station. She was sitting with a basket of wool on her lap.

'I'm supposed to be knitting something for the church bazaar, but can't decide what,' she told her.

'Mum knits Dad's socks, but he says they're a bit knobbly!' Kay laughed.

'What about you? Do you knit?'

'No, I'm useless at knitting and sewing. Mum used to make all my clothes when I was younger, and she does sometimes still make things for me. But she bought me a beautiful dress for when I go dancing.'

'That's what you like to do, then.'

'Yes, it is.' Kay was surprised at her reply. After George had left her she hadn't thought she'd be interested in dancing again, but now she realised she'd like to go regularly.

'I used to love to dance, too. My hip's a bit painful at the moment, but dancing was my passion when I was younger. It was all ballroom in those days, but you young ones have lots of new dances, like that Lindy Hop thing.'

'You must come with me some time, even if you sit out most of them and just watch. I'm sure you could waltz, though, and I'm happy to take the male part.'

'Are you saying I wouldn't be asked to dance by a man?' Olive pretended to be indignant. 'Although I certainly wouldn't get a partner as handsome as yours.'

Kay blushed. She supposed she could think of Michael as her dancing partner. She wondered if she should ask him to go with her again.

'The other thing I like doing is helping Dad in the garden. You said I could do what I like with yours. Do you mean it?'

'Definitely.'

'If it's all right with you I'd like to grow some vegetables and a few flowers for cutting. I'll have a think about the possibilities and tell you what I come up with. First I'll need to dig the vegetable patch over.'

'That sounds like hard work. Still, you're young and fit. And I've always thought hard work never hurt anyone.'

'What is it you're going to knit?'

'I think I'll stick to a child's jumper.' Olive started putting wool to one side, apparently intent on the job, but to Kay it looked as if she had something on her mind.

'Shall I make some cocoa?' Kay offered a little later, unable to suppress a yawn.

Olive glanced at the clock on the mantelpiece.

'You've had a long day, I was forgetting. Yes, cocoa would be nice. Thank you.'

Out in the kitchen, Kay found a small milk pan and set about making the bedtime drinks. She'd take hers upstairs, she decided.

Her bed was still cluttered and she'd need to sort out what she'd be wearing to the office in the morning. She'd also need to set her alarm clock; her mum had always made sure she was up in plenty of time in the mornings, but it was up to Kay now!

'Before you go up to bed, I'm going to say something.' Kay perched on the arm of a chair, waiting.

'Your friend and I had a little chat while you were out of the room this afternoon. I told him in no uncertain terms that I didn't trust the other solicitors in the town.

'They did have a good reputation and I used their services at one time, but more recently other people have said they've made mistakes and acted unethically. You know the ones I mean?'

Kay nodded, holding her breath, wondering what was coming next.

'Twigge and Moore. He was being tactful about them, remaining professional I expect, but let me give you a warning. You want to make sure you steer clear of them.'

Forged Signatures

Kay could smell delicious aromas of bacon and egg as she made her way downstairs, dressed in a crisp white blouse and a black skirt.

'Here you are, Kay. This should set you up for the day.' Olive set a steaming plate in front of her.

There were tomatoes, fried potatoes, bacon and two poached eggs. Kay tucked in and could barely manage a slice of toast and marmalade afterwards.

'That was wonderful, thank you.'

'Good. I want you to treat this as your home. There'll be no standing on ceremony. We must be honest with each other and say what we think. If you leave rings round the bath tub, I'll tell you!'

'That's fine by me.'

'And if you want to entertain your

friends here, you must. That Michael is a lovely man. I took to him straight away. I'll be very happy for you to invite him for a meal and you can use the sitting-room and watch the television if you like. I'm quite content in my chair in the kitchen. I don't watch television much anyway.'

'We haven't got one at home. Mum did talk about renting one, but she's never got round to it. The first time I watched was to see the coronation. We went to a neighbour's house. I thought it was very exciting.'

'There are some good programmes, and it's company when you're on your own. But I'm not alone now, so I don't suppose it will be switched on much.'

'I'm not sure about inviting Michael round, but I would like to invite a nice young girl from my old office. I'm very fond of Betty, and as she's not moving with us to Blayton, I thought it would be nice if she could visit.'

'There's a truckle bed in the attic. I'm sure we could put it up in your room when she comes. It'll be a bit of a squeeze, but you girls will manage.'

'That's kind of you. We'll have to see what her mum thinks, but if she agrees I could take her dancing. I think she'd enjoy that.' Kay glanced at her watch. 'I'll just nip up and clean my teeth then I'll be off.' She stood up and started clearing the plates.

'Don't worry about doing that. I've got all day to clear up. Your sandwiches and apple are on the table in the hall.'

'Thank you.'

Kay had plenty of time to get to the office, so she decided to stroll through the park. The green hills which had been shelters during the war looked as though they would be fun for children to play on.

As she passed the wooden hut two of the park keepers were sitting outside on a bench drinking their tea and having a smoke.

'Morning, miss.' One nodded at her. She smiled back and felt happy that her walk was so pleasant.

* * *

Kay spent the morning taking deliveries of furniture and stationery and enjoyed deciding where things should go. On one of his brief visits into the office that morning Michael had told her he would leave the arrangement of the office in her hands.

She was thrilled at the prospect of showing him what she'd achieved so far, but when he next appeared she could tell immediately that he wasn't in the best of moods. Knowing his last appointment had been with Tom Reacher, she wondered what this meant for the future of Harris and Partners, as they were now known.

'You won't believe what Tom told me,' he began as he sat rigidly in one of the new office chairs. 'They received a letter on our headed paper, typewritten and apparently from Dad. Tom showed it to me. Very convincing.'

'What did it say?'

'That, due to the downward turn

Tom Reacher's company was taking, we were no longer going to accept their business. It was quite horrible, and Tom couldn't believe Dad had written it. That's why, after he'd calmed down, he wanted to discuss things with me. We've always had a good relationship with them, and he felt the letter was quite out of character.'

'Who sent it? You said headed notepaper, didn't you? Remember the stationery that went missing!'

'Of course. You ought to be in an Agatha Christie novel!'

'I enjoy reading her books. I really like the Miss Marple ones. And I'd love to go to London to see 'The Mouse-trap'.' Kay realised that Michael had calmed down now that they were chatting about other things, but she was intrigued with this story. 'Do you think you know who stole the paper and wrote the letter?'

'I have a very good idea. You remember Charlie left the firm sud-denly? I won't tell you what had been going on, but as soon as I discovered what he'd been doing I fired him. I imagine he took the headed notepaper to write a reference, and then decided he'd get his own back on me by taking Reacher and Good's business away from us. I can't prove any of it, though. I'm just pleased that we've sorted it all out and got the business back again.'

Kay had a sudden desire to wrap her arms round him and comfort him. She remembered what Olive had said about inviting him back for a meal and to watch TV. She was painting a lovely picture in her head, of the two of them cuddling up together on Olive's settee, when she realised Michael was talking to her.

'You're in a dream again, Kay. I hope all this work isn't too much for you.'

'Not at all, I love being busy. I was just remembering something Olive said to me this morning.'

'How's that going?'

'Very well. I suppose we'd better get on.'

As she walked over to one of the desks she noticed something that had puzzled her earlier.

'I've just remembered something that might be relevant to that business with Charlie. We had the furniture we'd chosen from the old office delivered today so I cleaned out some of the drawers. In Charlie's old desk drawer I found something which I couldn't work out.' She grabbed a handful of paper. 'Look at this — practice signatures. I couldn't understand what it was all about. It must mean Charlie got a job with Twigge and Moore by writing a false reference and forging your father's signature.'

'I don't suppose they mind too much, especially if he causes our downfall. I wonder who else he'll write to, though, and what else he'll do.'

'We'll have to hope he feels he's done enough damage and leaves us alone from now on.'

As Michael didn't respond, she continued.

'If it's all right with you, I thought I'd

have my lunch and then explore the high street.'

Kay wondered if he would offer to go with her, but he simply nodded his head and went over to the filing cabinet in the corner.

Kay was delighted at the range of shops along the main street in Blayton. She bought two pairs of stockings and a pale pink Coty lipstick.

She'd spent a long time looking around the shops and decided to go back to the office to eat her lunch. There was still a lot to do there, and Michael might need someone to answer the telephone.

The news about Charlie had been a shock to her. He wasn't her favourite person, but she'd never thought he could be involved in anything dishonest. It was good that Michael had secured Reacher and Good's business again, but she must keep a vigilant eye on things in case any other clients had been similarly approached by Charlie Spencer.

Michael had disappeared from the outer office when Kay returned and she could hear him moving around in his room. A tap came at the door and when she answered it there was another delivery man on the doorstep asking her to sign yet another receipt.

'What is it?'

'A refrigerator.' He wheeled in a large cardboard box. 'Where do you want it?'

Kay had no idea.

'By the kettle, I imagine,' she improvised. 'I can always move it later.'

'It's heavy,' the man warned.

'Ah, it's come!' Michael appeared at Kay's side as she was peering inside the refrigerator.

'Betty would love this — no more sour milk! I must write and tell her all about it.'

'You're a good friend to have.' Michael gave her an admiring glance. 'Let's have a look at the plug. I'll need to put a fuse in.'

'I can do that,' Kay said confidently. Her father had taught her all sorts of useful things around the house.

'There should be a screwdriver around somewhere, but I've no idea where.' Michael looked around with a frown on his face.

'I've been putting together a box of useful things.' Kay pulled it out from under her desk and rummaged through it. 'See? Spare light bulbs, candles in case of a power cut and matches, of course, as well as fuses and fuse wire. Ah, here's the screwdriver.' She deftly fixed the fuse into place and plugged the refrigerator lead into the wall. It made a loud humming noise before settling down to a mesmeric whirr.

'Kay, you're a marvel, you really are. Where would I be without you?' He picked up his briefcase. 'I have to go out again, but I should be back before you leave. If not, what shall we do about locking up?'

'I suppose I should have a spare key to the office. But if you're going out it'll have to wait until tomorrow now. I'll wait until you get back before I leave.'

There was plenty to occupy Kay that afternoon and by the time Michael returned the office was looking very welcoming. The air smelt of lavender polish and Kay had arranged the furniture so that a client coming in would be able to view the staff and not just their backs hunched over their desks.

Staff! They'd need to recruit more people, of course. She was sure Michael had it in hand, but the only other person transferring from Harris and Son was one of the typists who had an aunt living in Blayton with whom she could lodge. Kay had spotted an agency a few doors along from Harris and Partners. She decided to ask Michael if she should enlist their help in finding accounting and clerical staff. Suddenly there seemed an awful lot still to do.

'You're not to worry about all of these things,' Michael insisted when she regaled him with the list of things which still needed to be done. 'I've not been idle. This afternoon I engaged the help of a friend. He has a list of people who I will arrange to interview during the week. We're not going to open for business yet, and Dad and I will also be having meetings with the two new partners we want to take on.'

'It will be fun having new work colleagues. Will we have a new junior?'

'I think that's the least of our worries right now, but yes, I would like to help another young person into work. Let's leave that until we're settled. You look tired, Kay. Why don't you take yourself off home? Let me give you a lift.'

'No, it's not far to walk and some fresh air will do me good.'

Arriving back at Elm Close, Kay felt wrung out. She had a wash in her room and changed into a pair of slacks and a clean blouse. Then she rinsed her stockings and hung them over the basin. It was lucky she'd bought fresh supplies today.

Her tummy growled in spite of her large breakfast and lunchtime sandwiches. It was nearly seven o'clock, so she went downstairs to the kitchen.

'Goodness, you look worn out, Kay. Busy day, I expect. Everything new.'

'We've got a fridge,' Kay told her. 'There's nothing in it yet, but it will be useful, especially if we have a hot summer.'

Olive nodded and started ladling stew into big round dishes.

'Don't wait for me.'

'This is delicious,' Kay said, tasting it, 'and the dumplings are so light. I wish I could cook like you and Mum.'

'I'll teach you, if you like.' Olive sat down opposite Kay. 'It's quite easy, really, if you stick to simple recipes to begin with.' They ate in silence for a while. 'I hope you don't mind eating in the kitchen.'

'Not at all. It's nice and cosy.'

After a blackberry and apple crumble with hot creamy custard, Kay pushed back her chair.

'I don't think I can move! If you're going to feed me like this every day I won't fit through the door!'

108

'I don't like anyone going hungry,' Olive said, getting up to clear the table.

'I'll do that.' Kay jumped to her feet.

The doorbell startled the two women.

'I don't get callers at this time in the evening,' Olive said, moving to answer it. 'I wonder who it could be.'

Kay stayed in the kitchen clearing up, as she was quite sure no-one would be calling on her.

Olive bustled in, followed by Michael.

'Kay, I'm sorry to barge in like this. It's just that I've had another key cut for the office.' He turned to Olive. 'Kay's been making her mark in the reception area. She's full of good ideas.'

'Have a seat. How about a dish of crumble with custard? It's still nice and hot,' Olive offered.

'That would be lovely, thank you.' Michael sat at the kitchen table, looking comfortable and relaxed.

'I told Kay she can invite her friends round, so I hope to see more of you.'

'That's very kind, but maybe Kay sees enough of me at work!' He tucked into the large portion of pudding.

Kay wasn't sure what to say.

'Olive says we can watch television some time, but I don't suppose that's something unusual for you.'

'I do have a television, but I don't watch much. It would be pleasant to come and watch a programme with you . . . and Olive.'

Olive winked at Kay, who decided she should put the kettle on to make tea. She listened to Michael and Olive chatting away to each other.

After the tea Michael said, 'I could stay here all evening, but I'd better be getting back. I'll see you in the morning, Kay.'

'I've had such a busy day I might oversleep and not turn up!'

'You had better. I need you!'

After Michael had left, Olive stretched her legs and rested them on the footstool she had in front of her armchair in the sitting-room.

'So he really needs you!'

'Well, I suppose I am quite an

110

efficient secretary,' Kay said, secretly pleased that Olive was teasing her.

'Did you see the look in those lovely blue eyes?'

Kay laughed.

'Do you think he's handsome?'

'Not like some of the film stars you see, but I think he's very attractive. What about you?' Olive delved down the side of the armchair and produced a bag of sweets. She held them out to Kay, who took one and popped it in her mouth.

'I haven't told anyone else this, but I think he's gorgeous!' Kay said, her cheeks bulging.

'I think he's got a soft spot for you. Why else would he turn up just to bring that key? It wasn't necessary. It was just an excuse. He'd be at work in the morning to let you in, wouldn't he?'

'I think he's kind, that's all. There's no way he'd consider me anything other than a friend. I'm sure he has plenty of admirers at the tennis club he goes to.'

'I don't know. I've seen the way he looks at you.'

Kay had a warm feeling inside as she got ready for bed. Perhaps it was possible that Michael could think of her as someone other than a friend.

The Old Boy Network

It was back to business the next day. Michael looked as though he'd been at the office for some time before Kay arrived. He'd thrown off his jacket, loosened his tie and undone the top buttons of his shirt.

'I want to discuss a few things with you, Kay. I've been thinking a lot about our relationship.'

Kay's heart missed a beat.

'I've decided that I must share everything with you completely. You've been my secretary for quite some time now, and I think you need to know all I do about our employees and clients. I'm relying on your discretion.' Michael took a deep breath. 'So, I'm going to start by telling you the whole story about Charlie Spencer.'

Kay scolded herself. What had she

been expecting? Some declaration of undying love?

'There have been discrepancies in the accounts over the past few months. At first the missing amounts were small and we put it down to accounting errors, but then the sums became larger so Dad and I decided I should keep a close eye on things. I went over the accounts with a fine tooth comb. What I found was that Charlie was fiddling them. I asked him to stay on after everyone else had gone home one day, and challenged him about it.'

'That must have been awful.'

'It was. I don't know what you think of Charlie, but he is a very unpleasant character. When I confronted him he sneered and said it was no more than his due. He said a lot of other disagreeable things which I won't bore you with. I fired him there and then and told him to collect his belongings from his desk. That is probably when he took the stationery from the cupboard. Realising he wouldn't get a reference from me he thought he would write his own on our paper. That's what I guess, anyway. And of course he wrote that letter to Reacher and Good.'

'Shouldn't you tell Twigge and Moore?'

'I'll definitely let them know I didn't write his reference and also that I fired him for fiddling our accounts. You'll have to make sure the letter is marked as confidential. We're going to have to be very careful about any further damage he might inflict on us, but with you here by my side I'm sure we can get through this and build the business.'

'Good morning.' A man had walked into the office without knocking. 'I hope you don't mind me calling unexpectedly. I was just passing so thought I'd see how things are going.' He held out his hand to a puzzled Michael. 'Alastair Barnes from Twigge and Moore.'

Kay and Michael exchanged a private look, then Kay shook hands with Alastair. His clasp was weak and his touch damp; she didn't take to him at all.

'How about a cup of tea for one of our potential new partners?' Michael suggested.

Kay left the room and, having taken the two men tea and biscuits, started her day's work. She thought that Michael must have taken leave of his senses to contemplate having someone from Twigge and Moore as a partner. It wasn't long before Michael was ushering his visitor into the outer office and taking his leave of him.

'So this is where all the real action's going to take place,' Alastair said, sitting on Kay's desk and staring down at her.

'I'm afraid I am very busy at the moment and don't have time to chat.' Kay continued with her typing.

'You should be nice to me. My father plays golf with Michael's dad.'

That explained it. The old boy network. Kay was angry. She thought that people should get jobs on merit, not by whom they knew. She'd thought better of Michael! She took a deep breath. This horrible man would be out of the office very soon.

'No ring on your finger. Are you spoken for?'

'That's none of your business.'

'Fiery, aren't you?'

'Not especially, but I do have work to do. Please go back to your work, and leave me to get on with mine.'

'You might regret your attitude when I'm a partner here.' He chuckled. 'How about going out for lunch today? Maybe we could get to know each other better.'

'Thank you, but I'm working through lunch. Now, I have to take letters in to be signed.'

She picked up the papers and left him gaping after her.

'He's insufferable!' Kay slammed the papers down in front of Michael, who grabbed her wrist.

'Hey, calm down!'

She pulled away and stood looking out of the window. He immediately joined her.

'What's wrong? What did he say?'

'Just that his father knows yours, and would I go out with him? What an awful man.'

'That doesn't sound so bad, Kay. His father does know my father and what single man wouldn't ask you out?' Michael stroked her arm. 'The more I get to know you, the more I like you. If only . . .'

Kay was still cross and pulled away.

'I don't understand how you can even consider someone from Twigge and Moore. I'll tell you something. If he becomes one of the partners, I'm leaving!' She flounced out of the room.

The day didn't improve and by the time she went back to Olive's in the evening she was wondering if she'd made a huge mistake moving to Blayton.

Olive had made cottage pie for their evening meal, but Kay found she couldn't do justice to it nor face the jam roly poly for afters.

'What's wrong? Was it a bad day?'

'Dreadful.' Kay explained what had happened and how she wasn't sure Michael was quite the man she'd thought. 'If that awful Alastair is taken on I'm leaving the firm.'

'I'm sure Michael will choose the best person, rather than someone known by the family. He seems an honest, genuine man. I wouldn't worry. Now, come on, you must eat some of this roly poly, I made it just for you. I'm sorry if the meals I'm giving you are too heavy for this warm weather, but I never feel salad is enough when you've been at work all day.'

Kay forced herself to eat a few spoonsful, and when she found it was delicious and she was hungry she wolfed it down.

★　★　★

As clients wouldn't be appearing yet, Kay decided to wear more casual clothes to work which made the physical jobs a little easier. Her favourite outfit was tapered slacks with a loose fitting blouse and a patent leather belt along with flat shoes. She tied her hair back in a high pony tail and liked the way it bounced when she walked.

One day Michael watched her arrive at work and told her how lovely she looked.

Kay was flattered.

'I'm surprised you notice. You've got far too much to do to be looking at what your staff wear.'

'You're not just staff,' he said, before hurriedly shutting himself back in his office.

Kay didn't know what to make of him sometimes, but she stayed in an exceptionally good mood all day.

It was almost a week later when Olive took an envelope from her pocket.

'This came for you in the second post.'

'It's from Betty.' Delighted, Kay ripped at the envelope wanting to read what her friend had to tell her.

'Dear Kay, I am having a nice time working for Mr Harris Senior, I expect you are with Mr Michael, too. I have been for an interview. I felt very scared, but the man was kind and put me at my ease. I am looking forward to visiting you one day. Will I see Mr Michael? I have something to tell you about Charlie. I hope you won't be cross. I'll tell you everything when I see you. Love Betty.'

As Kay folded the letter back into the envelope, she frowned.

'I'm worried about her getting mixed up with Charlie. I wonder what it is she has to tell me and why would I be cross? Oh, Betty, what have you done?'

Usually Kay was pleased to see Michael in the office when she arrived, but the next day she had other things on her mind. She hadn't slept well and had woken with a headache.

Before taking off her jacket, she filled the kettle and set it to boil. She placed the milk bottle from the front step into the fridge along with her sandwiches in their paper bag.

'Kay, good morning.' Michael came out of his office. 'Ah, you've got the kettle on. Good. We have a new member of staff joining us in a few minutes.'

'Oh? Who would that be then? Someone else from Twigge and Moore?' Kay's tone surprised even her and she blushed. 'I'm sorry, Michael, you don't deserve to be on the end of my acid tongue today.' She tried to smile at him.

He perched on the desk and patted her shoulder.

'I know there's an awful lot to do around here and you're single-handed. I'd like to help, but I've done the next best thing. I thought a receptionist would be the answer. There, what do you think?'

Kay wasn't sure what she thought.

'Thank you, Michael,' she managed. 'Do you want me to sit in on the interview? What's her name, and what time is her appointment?' Kay pulled the office diary towards her and held her pencil poised over the page.

Michael stood up.

'I don't think you understand. She's starting work. Today. I've already engaged her.'

'I see.' Kay was determined to stay calm. 'In that case, I'll be pleased to show her around the office and go through the routine with her. Would you like a cup of tea now, or wait until she gets here?'

'Shall we wait until Vanessa arrives and have it together?'

There were a million questions coursing through Kay's mind, but she felt she couldn't ask any of them without seeming bad-tempered and ungrateful.

'How did you hear about Vanessa? Was it through an agency or a business contact of yours?'

'No, nothing like that. She belongs to the tennis club and was asking about jobs. I'm sure you and she will get on. She's very different from most of the others at the club. Come along one day.

We could arrange a game.'

Kay laughed.

'I'm not sure about that.'

'I thought we'd already agreed. You teaching me to dance and me giving you a bit of instruction with tennis.'

'But you could already dance,' Kay protested. 'My tennis isn't even as far up as the most basic level!'

Already Kay was feeling happier. She and Michael had their old rapport back. She couldn't blame him for trying to help her. It had previously been agreed that more staff were needed.

He disappeared into his room and Kay stood up, hung her jacket on the coat stand and consulted the drawing she'd made of the office furniture and the space it was to occupy. Just a few more changes to be made.

The office door flew open and an attractive young woman came confidently up to Kay.

'I'm Vanessa,' she said. 'Mike's expecting me. Would you tell him I'm here?'

'Of course.'

Kay was not taking to this forthright young woman at all. She was about to invite her politely to take a seat, when she saw that she had already done so.

Michael came bounding out to the reception area, grinning at Vanessa.

'How good of you to get here this morning,' he enthused. 'Would you bring us some tea, Kay?'

The two of them disappeared to Michael's office, leaving Kay wondering what had happened to the suggestion that they would all have their tea together. Still, it was nothing to do with her. She was not the owner of the business and she had other things to do.

During the day Kay reluctantly had to admit that Vanessa was efficient as well as attractive. After being shown how the telephone transfers took place, she'd sent a couple of calls to Michael's office and had deflected another two or three by taking messages and passing them on.

She also liked to chat.

'Isn't it good that Mike's going to be the boss? I think he'll be ever so successful. The girls at the tennis club think he'll want to settle down soon, because he'll need a wife to put on business dinners, host cocktail evenings and so on.'

'I'm sure you're right,' Kay said, hoping that if she didn't join in, Vanessa would be quiet and let her concentrate. She was working through the invoices, trying to make things add up.

'Why don't you nip out to the bakers and get some buns then make tea?' Kay really didn't want anything to eat, as the lunch Olive provided was more than adequate.

'That's not a good idea, Kay. I don't want to put on weight and I'm sure you need to watch yours, too. We don't want Mike getting chubby, either. I'll just get myself a glass of water.'

Kay sighed and tried to ignore the endless chatter. She supposed she'd get used to Vanessa, but today she couldn't wait for six o'clock to come round.

'It's fun to be working for Mike,' Vanessa said at half past five.

She fetched her coat from the coat stand and shrugged it on. Kay didn't know what to say. If Vanessa had been an ordinary employee she'd have reminded her of the agreed hours, but she was Michael's friend and so she kept quiet.

Having spent another hour typing more letters Michael had dictated that day, Kay was ready to go home. Just as she was about to head back to Olive's he appeared with a pile of papers in his hand.

'I thought you could file these before you go.'

Kay was cross once again.

'Why don't you ask your pretty new receptionist to file them in the morning? It's not as if she's fully employed.'

Michael was quiet for a moment, then spoke.

'Really, Kay, I'm disappointed you feel that way. I thought better of you.'

Doing the Stroll

'Sorry I'm late, Olive. I had to stay and work on for a bit. I hope the meal's not spoilt.'

'Not to worry. I've been to my friend's house for a natter so I thought we'd get fish and chips tonight. You like them, don't you?' Olive took her purse from the table and waited for Kay's response.

'Yes, I do, but let me go.'

'No, I need to keep active and I like a chat with the owners. You put some plates to warm in the oven and lay the table. Then make a cup of tea. Salt and vinegar?'

'Please.'

It wasn't long before Olive returned, with Michael trailing behind her.

'Look who I found at the chip shop! The poor man was going to take fish and chips back to the office because he has so much work to do.'

'That's right, I had some filing to see to.' Michael grinned.

'Filing? You shouldn't be doing that.'

'I know, but some members of my staff have minds of their own.' He winked at Kay and mouthed, 'Sorry.'

Kay couldn't stay cross with him. She unwrapped the newspaper from her portion and breathed in the delicious aroma as it wafted into the room.

'They look good. I'm starving.' Kay tucked in. 'We had fish and chips every Friday at home.'

'You must miss your family. You don't regret coming to Blayton, do you?' Michael asked.

'Not at all. I'm very happy here — when you're not being a slave driver, and when your new receptionist manages to stop talking for a few minutes!'

'She is a bit of a chatterbox. Would it be a help if you moved your desk into my office? I'm pretty quiet when I'm working. It would be nice.'

Kay wished she could just say, 'Yes,

that would be wonderful,' but she knew it wouldn't be professional.

'I will be fine. I'll get used to Vanessa, and she'll be busier and have more people to talk to soon. Now, if everyone has finished I'll put the paper in the bin and make some more tea.'

That night sleep was eluding Kay, and she knew why. Michael was always in her thoughts, even though she knew her feelings for him weren't reciprocated. She went over the evening. She remembered the moment when his hand had brushed hers. How lovely it would be to move into his office. If only . . .

Kay gave herself a talking to. She must separate work and her home life. She needed to pursue her hobbies and get to know new people. Tomorrow she would ask Olive about the possibilities for dancing in the town. There was the Orchid Ballroom, of course, but she wouldn't want to go there on her own. She'd find out about classes and maybe learn one of the new dances!

Having made the decision she turned over yet again and promptly fell asleep.

★   ★   ★

Olive admired the green and pink dress Kay was wearing.

'You look lovely. You'll be the belle of the ball!'

'Don't stay up, will you? I won't be very late, but I expect it will be past your bedtime. Did I tell you that tonight we're going to learn a dance called the Stroll? I think I know a little bit of it. Come on, Olive, let's try, It's a simple six count. I'm not sure, but it might go like this. Tap, tap, tap, step, break, step. And again.'

When Olive had collapsed in her armchair Kay grabbed her bag and skipped towards the door.

'I'll teach you properly when I've learned all the steps.'

'I can't wait!' Olive grinned as she caught her breath.

When Kay arrived at the venue, it wasn't quite what she'd been expecting. It was a plain wooden hall which wasn't nearly as glamorous as the Orchid Ballroom. Kay hoped the whole evening wouldn't be a big disappointment, and as soon as she walked in she was pleasantly surprised by the friendliness of the people there.

A tall, thin man, who introduced himself as Len, stood in the centre of the hall.

'Welcome to you all, especially any new members.' It seemed to Kay that all eyes were on her and she felt a bit shy. 'As usual, we'll walk through the steps before going on to practise them with music. Just follow me.'

He turned his back on the gathering and took them through their paces a couple of times. Then he put a crackly record on the gramophone and the music echoed out.

For Kay, it was much easier to move with the music as it transported her. When the music stopped, there were several admiring glances in her direction.

'You've danced before,' Len said.

'Not the Stroll, but yes, I used to dance. Although I haven't for a while. Not like this.'

'You're a natural,' he said. 'Everybody, find a partner, one you've not danced with before. That way you get to know each other. We're one man short, so I'll dance this week. You've done well with the new routine, but we'll return to the old tried and trusted ones now, shall we?'

Kay found she was dancing with a pleasant young man who trod on her toes and clasped her too tightly. But she didn't mind. It was good to be on the dance floor again.

After an hour had passed, Kay felt hot and her feet ached a bit with the unaccustomed movements.

'Tea break!' Len called.

'I could do with something a bit stronger than tea,' one of the men gasped.

'Me, too,' a young woman added, fanning herself with her hand. 'Are we going for a drink afterwards, as usual?'

'Yes. You must come with us, Kay. It's nice to have another woman in the group.'

When they'd had their tea, Len put on another record and invited them to take their partners for a waltz.

'That's an easy one for you all to enjoy,' he said.

The evening passed pleasantly and Kay was sorry to leave the hall, but was looking forward to going to the pub along the road with the group. She was making new friends and it felt good.

'Kay, I forgot to say that there's a competition soon,' Len said. 'Would you like me to enter you?'

She had no hesitation in nodding her head.

'I'll let you have the details next week.'

At last she was starting to achieve her independence.

Kay was surprised to see the lights on

in Elm Close when she arrived home. She let herself in quietly in case Olive was asleep in her chair. Tiptoeing into the sitting room, she was greeted with a smile from her landlady.

'I had to wait up and see how you got on,' she said standing up. 'The milk's in the pan. Come through to the kitchen and tell me all about it.'

'It was great fun,' Kay enthused, keeping Olive amused with the goings on of the evening while the milk boiled. 'And we went to the pub!'

'You sound as if I'd be shocked.'

'And you're not?' Kay knew her mother would be.

'Not at all.'

Olive Carter was full of surprises, Kay thought again as she sipped her cocoa. It was nearly midnight, and Kay was pleased that tomorrow was Saturday and she didn't have to set her alarm clock. Up in her room she pirouetted lightly around the room, her pretty dress circling around her. She'd drift off to sleep easily tonight, she reflected.

But once in bed with the quietness of the night around her, Kay found her thoughts returning to Michael. A lot had happened in the past few days. When she closed her eyes all she could see was Michael and Vanessa laughing together, and she was excluded.

The next morning, when Kay eventually wandered down to the kitchen in her dressing gown to fetch a cup of tea Olive insisted she tell her every last detail of the previous evening once again. Kay watched her landlady baking.

'That fruit cake mix looks delicious.'

'You can lick the bowl out when I've put the mixture in the tin,' Olive said before checking the temperature of the oven.

As Kay was scraping the sides of the bowl with a spoon she remembered Michael saying that they hadn't ordered a cake for his dad's retirement do.

'Do you ever bake cakes for other people?'

'Sometimes people ask me. I do a few

iced Christmas cakes for friends.'

'Would you be happy to make the retirement cake for Michael's dad? You'll be paid for it.'

'I'd love to. Just let me have enough to cover the cost of the ingredients. When you're dressed we'll go to the grocer's and get what we need.'

⋆　⋆　⋆

The weekend had been hectic. After getting the shopping Olive had continued to make cakes on Saturday while Kay busied herself with a bit of housework, and on Sunday they'd walked around the park and up and down the high street with Olive showing Kay the points of interest. Even with all that activity, Olive's hip had still allowed her to cook an extremely mouth-watering Sunday lunch of roast beef with all the trimmings, with an apple pie and custard for pudding.

But now it was Monday morning and Kay made sure she was in the office early as it would be open officially for business today from ten o'clock. There was no sign of Vanessa and Kay decided not to mention her absence.

'Hello, Kay. Good weekend?' Michael asked, following her in.

'Very nice, thanks. I hope yours was, too.' Kay wondered what he'd been doing, but didn't like to ask.

He just smiled at her.

'Where's Vanessa?'

'Not in yet. How far does she have to come?'

'I gave her a lift. She asked me to drop her at the front door before I parked the car. I thought she'd be at her desk by now. It doesn't matter, she won't be long.'

Kay tried hard not to feel jealousy at Vanessa being given a lift to work by Michael. The telephone rang and Kay hurried to answer it, picking up a pencil to jot down a message.

Luckily, the recruiting of more office staff had been easier than Kay had imagined. Apart from Vanessa there would be two typists and two accounting staff starting that morning.

There was a gentle tap at the door and when it opened, Kay ended her phone call.

'Susan, how lovely to see you! Come on in and inspect the new office. I'm so pleased I'm not the only one who transferred here.'

Susan had been a very efficient typist at the offices of Harris and Son, and had an aunt in Blayton with whom she could lodge during the working week.

'Which is my desk? Is Mr Michael in? We have missed him.' Susan hung up her jacket and put her bag in the drawer of the desk Kay indicated she would occupy. 'By the way, Betty sends her best wishes. She says she's written you a letter. She can't wait to visit you. We haven't seen hide nor hair of Charlie Spencer.'

'He's working for a rival firm here in Blayton,' said Kay, hoping she hadn't said too much, but it would be general knowledge around the town and Susan

139

might bump into him.

The door opened again and the other new employees sidled in and Kay gave them her attention, showing them their places and introducing Susan.

At one minute before ten o'clock Vanessa arrived, looking cool and serene.

'Just been to have my hair done,' she explained. 'It's a big day, isn't it? Opening a new office.' She glanced at Kay's hair quickly before adding, 'Well, I'm the receptionist and I'm the first person a client sees, so I have to make a good impression.'

If you're around to make one, Kay seethed to herself. There was no time for introductions as Michael came out of his office. He immediately walked over to Vanessa. Typical, Kay thought to herself, but then she heard what he was saying.

'I expect you'll be working through your lunch hour to make up for your lateness, Vanessa. Right now I'd like you to make tea for us all. As soon as it's ready let me know. I'm going to welcome everyone and explain a few things.' As he walked back to his office he winked at Kay.

For the next ten minutes Kay could hear the loud rattling of crockery and slamming of cupboard doors.

The rest of the week passed quickly as there was a lot of interest generated by the new firm, with potential clients popping in to get copies of their terms of business.

Two new partners had taken up their positions and were often huddled in meetings with Michael, occasionally requiring Kay to come and take shorthand notes to be typed up.

The office was a hive of activity.

'How are you getting on with the other partners?' Michael asked during a slack moment.

'I like them. But I was surprised that Alastair wasn't asked to join you, if only because he's known to your family.'

Michael put his arm around her.

'I think you took a dislike to him, and I don't want you working in an environment where you feel threatened and uncomfortable.'

* * *

On Friday morning Michael made an announcement.

'I know that several of you weren't employees at the old office, but I'd like to invite everybody to my father's retirement party this afternoon. I've arranged for a mini bus to take everyone. It'll be ready to leave at two o'clock.'

He walked over to Kay's desk.

'Kay, will you come with me in my car? I need to go a bit earlier to check that everything's just right, and you always spot things that haven't been thought of.'

'Yes, of course.'

She noticed Vanessa glaring at her. Kay had tried very hard to be friendly with her, but it was hard work and she was beginning to feel it wasn't worth it.

'Mike!' Vanessa called.

'Yes, what is it?'

'Could I have a word? It's just that I get sick in mini buses and I'd really like to go to this party. It's such an important occasion and I feel so loyal to this firm and your family.'

'Sorry. My car's a two-seater, and I've already asked Kay to come with me.'

Vanessa gave him a woeful look.

'All right. I'm sure Kay won't mind going with the others.' He turned to her. 'Is that OK if I take Vanessa in the car?'

Kay tried to suppress her feelings.

'Fine,' she said, banging away at her typewriter.

So much for Michael saying that he wanted her help. He'd have to rely on Vanessa now.

A Tennis Lesson

It was great fun in the mini bus. Susan started singing and soon everyone was joining in. They were all still laughing and giggling as they wandered into the outer office which had been decorated with streamers and balloons. As expected, the table was laden with plates piled high with delicious-looking food. Michael was opening champagne.

Betty bounced over.

'What do you think, Kay?' she asked indicating the food.

'Mrs Harris has done us proud as usual.'

Betty beamed.

'It wasn't Mrs Harris. She was too busy organising some charity event at the golf club.'

'Who sorted all this lot out, then? Mr Harris's secretary has left already.'

'I did!'

'That's wonderful! You should be really pleased with yourself.' Yet another achievement for the girl; she was doing really well. 'Betty, what was it you wanted to tell me about Charlie?'

'I met Charlie as I was leaving the office one evening. I think maybe he'd been hanging around waiting for me. He told me how pretty I looked, and how he'd always had a soft spot for me. He asked if he could walk me home and we chatted about this and that. When we got to my house he said how nice it was to see me again and how he'd like to take me out, and would I like to go out for dinner with him to that posh restaurant in Blayton. He was ever so charming. I told him I'd like to go out with him very much and that I'd ask my mum.'

'What did she say?'

'I didn't ask Mum, in the end. When I got to the door I turned round and really looked at him. There was something about him that told me he couldn't care less about me. I can't explain it. I called after him and told him my answer was no. What do you think he was up to?'

'I'm not sure. He's done some bad things, Betty. Maybe he was hoping to get some information from you about the business.'

'But why? He's got a good job at Twigge and Moore.'

'Let's forget Charlie. We don't want him to spoil this afternoon. You did the right thing. And don't worry, one day you'll have a lovely boyfriend.'

'I'm glad I refused him. Here, have this plate and help yourself.'

Kay wasn't quite sure where to start. There was an amazing array of small eats including sandwiches, cheese and pineapple on sticks and mushroom and salmon vol au vents.

Then she remembered the cake. If Michael had forgotten to bring it someone would have to go back to Blayton to fetch it. How on earth had she managed not to think of that? She supposed it was because her thoughts had been on other things, namely Vanessa and Michael. At least she'd remembered the gift and the card. Now all she had to do was get the last few people to sign it.

But first she needed to find out about the cake. She made her way over to Michael.

'Here, Kay, have some champagne. Wasn't it generous of Dad to buy this for us? It's a good one.' He studied the label of the bottle he was holding.

'I'm sure it is, and it was generous of you, too, to make such a large donation towards the binoculars we've given him. Michael, did you remember the cake?'

'Of course. That is, Vanessa reminded me.'

'She does have her uses, then.'

As soon as she saw Michael's face Kay wished the words back in her mouth.

He took her hand.

'Now listen to me. I don't know why you and she don't get on, but I want my office to be a happy one where everyone works together and supports each other. So, tell me, what's the problem?'

Kay drew in a breath.

'She takes advantage of her friendship with you. Her time-keeping is dreadful, and she doesn't pull her weight so she's creating tension with the rest of us. But you just don't seem able to see it, because she's your friend.'

'Nothing else?'

There was certainly nothing else that she was going to tell him. She pulled her hand out of his grip.

'There are a few more people who need to sign the card.' As she walked away from Michael she bumped into his dad and swiftly hid the card behind her back.

'Kay, how lovely to see you! I hear from Michael that everything is running smoothly in Blayton, and it's all down to you, according to him. He barely stops singing your praises. Apparently he feels more confident moving the business forward with you helping him.

'And now I've said too much, and

you're blushing. I was saying to Mrs H. the other day that we must have you round for Sunday lunch.'

'That would be lovely,' was all she could say.

Olive's cake was delicious and everyone had second helpings except for Vanessa who, after forking a small piece into her mouth, declared herself to be full.

Mr Harris was delighted with his binoculars and he stood at the window staring out through them. As Kay watched, Mrs Harris edged her way over to her husband. In a reflex action he put his arm around her shoulders and she relaxed against him.

Kay had never seen this side of him before and found it delightful. She just wished she'd find that sort of happiness.

Kay moved away to talk to people and then she glanced at the clock on the wall. Not wanting to interrupt Michael as he chatted, she waited for an opportune moment.

He turned to her with an easy smile. 'Did you want me, Kay?'

'I don't want to appear rude, but do you think it would be possible for me to slip away for a half an hour? I'd like to drop in on my parents now that I'm here.'

'Of course. Hang on, I'll give you a lift. It'll be good to see them again.'

Mr and Mrs Watson were delighted to see Kay, who'd brought them a piece of Olive's cake.

'If her cooking's like this, I'm sure you're in good hands. Oh, we do miss you, but your letters keep us up to date. And Dad says we might be able to have a telephone installed, so you can ring us up.'

Michael sipped tea while Kay nattered with her parents. Then she said her goodbyes and climbed into the car beside Michael to go back to the office, where the minibus would take her back to Blayton.

As Michael opened the car door for her, he said, 'We could go for a walk this evening when we get back, if you like. You deserve to relax for a while, after all the effort you've put in on the firm's behalf lately.'

The offer was tempting, but, 'I'm sorry, Michael, I've plans for this evening.'

'Doing something with Olive, are you?'

'I'm going dancing.'

'Not with George, I hope?'

Kay wasn't sure what to make of Michael's remark.

'I don't see what that's got to do with you.'

Sorry later, she sought him out later to apologise, but he was amongst a group of people and it didn't seem appropriate. Quite why she'd behaved like that, she wasn't sure. He didn't always bring out the best in her.

★ ★ ★

'Olive, it was the best office party I've been to. Your cake was very well received and I took a slice over to Mum and Dad. Do you think you could teach me to bake like that?'

Olive laughed.

'We'll see. Now, you'd better hurry if you're not going to be late for the dance class.'

'Coming with me?' Kay was heading for the stairs.

'Not this week,' Olive replied, taking a sweet from her pocket and popping it into her mouth.

'Hello, Kay!' the others greeted her as she hurried into the hall. 'We thought you might not be coming.'

'There was an office party I couldn't miss. I'll have to dance off the huge amount I ate!'

'I was just about to announce the competition,' Len said. 'It's going to take place at the Guildhall here in Blayton. We'll need to practise. During the tea break we'll discuss who's interested. I think I'd like to have a go myself.'

Kay felt herself unwinding as she

moved to the music, enjoying the different rhythms from the valeta waltz to the quick step. In the break, she chatted to the others about the forthcoming competition and resolved to enlist Olive's help as a partner.

The second half of the evening was very lively, with Len assuring everyone that jive was the latest thing. There was much laughter as they all tried to master the moves he put them through. It was a fun time and Kay enjoyed herself thoroughly. She realised she'd given Michael no thought. But now she wondered if he'd extended his invitation to Vanessa as she had turned him down. She was determined not to spoil a lovely day with negative thoughts.

The following day Kay discussed the garden with Olive and showed her the drawings she'd made.

'Looks like a lot of hard work, but as it's not me who's going to be doing it, I don't think I'll complain!' Olive studied the paper Kay put in front of her. 'Are you sure you can manage all of this?'

'I can try.' Kay hoped she wasn't going to be taking on too much. She was pleased at the way her life was turning out, with the new job, dancing classes and the garden, and was determined to make a success of it.

'Shall we go out and look at the plot and see where I hope to grow the different vegetables? It's a beautiful day, it seems criminal to stay indoors.'

Olive headed for the back door.

'You're good for me,' she said. 'I like to be on the move and have things going on.'

After they'd decided what could go where, Kay changed into old clothes. She then went to Olive's shed at the bottom of the garden where she found ancient tools which would have to do the job. Perhaps next time she went home she would be able to bring some of her dad's smaller implements, which would make the work a bit easier. The ground was hard as there hadn't been much rain, and it took a great deal of effort to turn the soil.

She was surprised to see Olive beckoning to her. Hoping for a cup of something hot or cold, she was even more surprised to see Michael making himself at home in the kitchen.

'Is everything all right?' Kay wondered what could have brought him here on a Saturday.

'I wanted to thank Olive for the cake she made for Dad. He had a wonderful time at the party.'

Olive chuckled.

'I'm glad everything went off all right. Kay's a good organiser, isn't she? I'll leave you two to chat while I go to the shop for a few things.'

'It was good of you to thank Olive. Would you like tea?'

'No thanks, I was on my way to the tennis club. That's another reason why I called in. I wanted to invite you to play tomorrow afternoon. What do you say?'

'I'd like to very much, thank you.'

Michael moved towards her and gently wiped her cheek with his hand.

'Your face is muddy.'

As he dabbed at her face, Kay gazed into his beautiful eyes, hoping the moment would last for a very long time. All too soon he dropped his hand, grinned and told her what time he'd booked the court for the next day.

It was only after the arrangements had been made and Michael had gone that Kay felt she had probably made a mistake accepting his invitation. For one thing, there was Vanessa. She wasn't sure she wanted to spend an afternoon watching their receptionist flirt with the boss.

★   ★   ★

She chose a light pair of shorts and a loose, white, short-sleeved blouse. Having put on her plimsolls she swung a cardigan round her shoulders and was ready.

'Do you think I look the part, Olive?'

Olive nodded admiringly.

'You look very pretty, Kay. Michael will be totally distracted from his game.

I'm sure you'll enjoy the afternoon.'

'I'm hopeless at tennis.' Kay sighed.

When she walked into the tennis club she hoped she looked more confident than she felt. She glanced round quickly to see where Michael was, but there was no sign of him.

Vanessa came up wearing a pretty tennis dress.

'Welcome to the club. Mike told me he was bringing you. I'm afraid he's not here yet. Let me get you a glass of lemonade whilst you're waiting.'

Vanessa carried three drinks over to a corner of the room where a young man was sitting, fast asleep.

'This is my fiancé. I'm afraid we were out at a party until late last night. Never mind him, I need to talk to you.'

It was hard to take all of this in! It seemed that Vanessa was engaged to the man snoring opposite her, and she was being surprisingly friendly.

'When I saw you walk in just now, you seemed like another person. What I mean is, at the office I'm really in awe of you. You're so efficient and in control! I know I'm a bit dizzy and I know you haven't taken to me.'

Kay felt awful for the way she'd behaved towards Vanessa. She was aware that she had been quite simply jealous.

'I'm sorry I didn't welcome and help you as much as I should have done, Vanessa. You do wonderfully well welcoming people to the office and answering the telephone. You're the right person for the job. I just wish your time-keeping was a bit better!'

Both girls laughed and the ice was broken.

'I'm glad to see you looking after Kay for me.' Michael appeared, wearing long white shorts and a cable knit sleeveless jumper over a sports shirt. 'Are you ready?'

Kay jumped up and followed him out to an empty court. After a knock about, Michael walked round to Kay's side of the court to give her a few hints on serving. He stood behind her and held both her arms as he showed her how to serve properly. Kay was aware of his body being close to hers and quite unable to concentrate on hitting the ball. After several tries she laughed and turned round to face him.

'You see, I'm hopeless at tennis!'

'You'll soon learn.' He leaned forward and kissed her on the forehead.

Just at that moment Vanessa was walking past and clapped.

'At last! It's time you two got together.'

'Silly girl,' Michael said. 'Come on, let's have another go.'

Even in her eyes, Kay seemed to be improving a bit by the time another club member came over and asked Michael for a game. He looked at Kay quizzically.

'It's fine by me. I'd like to watch.' She didn't pay much attention to the techniques of the two men as she was mesmerised by Michael. From what she could see there wasn't an ounce of fat on his body. His legs were strong and muscular and his serves were powerful.

The sun had come out from behind the clouds and was beating fiercely down on the court. Both men were sweating as they put all their efforts into winning. At last it was over and Michael admitted defeat.

'I'm going to change,' he called to Kay before stripping off his shirt, wiping his face with it and heading towards the gents' block.

Kay watched. His back was gleaming and muscular and she couldn't take her eyes from him.

A Warning

The atmosphere at the office was much lighter now that the tension between Kay and Vanessa had eased. During the break she joined Vanessa at her desk.

'I think I might join the tennis club,' she told her.

'That would be good. I know Mike doesn't like all the people there, but most of us are all right. Sorry about my fiancé. You'll like him when you meet him properly. Maybe sometime we could have a game of doubles.'

'I think that will be a long time in the future.' Kay sipped her tea.

'We all thought Mike'd be married by now. He's quite a catch. I think he's concentrating on his career. He once told me it was the most important thing to him. His parents made a lot of sacrifices for him when he was a young boy, and he's very keen to pay them back by making a success of the family business. Now his father's retired and Mike's branched out on his own, I think he's more than proved himself. He's such a loyal son.'

Kay didn't say anything, just let her new friend rattle on.

'We've all noticed the way he looks at you and how he pays you so much attention. Will he be inviting you to the tennis club summer dinner dance?'

'He hasn't said anything and I haven't heard about it.'

The telephone rang and Vanessa gave her usual cheery greeting. But then her face fell.

'But why? I don't understand. Do you think you should talk to Mr Harris before making the decision? His secretary is here now. Please have a word with her.' Then she looked at the receiver. 'He hung up.'

'Who was it?'

'Grant Brothers. They're taking their business to Twigge and Moore. He didn't say why, except that they'd heard something they didn't like.'

'I'd better tell Michael. I think we both know who's behind this and it's got to stop.' She went into his office.

Kay had never seen Michael look so angry.

'I'm going round to tackle Charlie Spencer. If he carries on, we're going to be losing all our business.'

'Are you sure it is him?'

'What do you think?'

'I think it almost certainly is, but we aren't absolutely sure, are we?'

'I could start by mentioning the signatures we found in his desk. We still have them as evidence. I can't leave this any longer. The business is at stake. But I'd like you to come with me. I need a witness and also, with you there, I won't overstep the mark and punch him!'

★ ★ ★

The meeting with Charlie at Twigge and Moore didn't go as Kay had thought it would. She found she was trembling as she followed Michael along the High Street to their rivals' office. Charlie greeted them warily and Mr Twigge ushered them into his room.

Of course, Charlie denied all knowledge of trying to poach clients from Harris and Partners and Mr Twigge was adamant that they had so many clients they could hardly keep up with the demand.

Charlie was very scathing when confronted with the signatures, stating that anyone could have written them and planted them in a desk drawer.

Naturally Mr Twigge defended his employee and suggested that Michael could have been mistaken. As they left, Kay turned to see Charlie's gloating smile.

Feeling that they hadn't achieved their objective, Kay was pleased to hear Michael raise his voice.

'Charlie Spencer, if I ever have cause to face you like this again, I will inform the authorities immediately. Do you understand? Consider yourself warned.'

The walk back to Harris and Partners was made in silence, but when they arrived on familiar territory, Michael said, 'Come with me, Kay.'

Together they headed for his room and collapsed in chairs.

'We need a break from this tension. Will you have dinner with me this evening?'

'I'll have to get in touch with Olive to let her know I won't be eating at home, but yes, please, I'd like that. Thank you.'

'You're seeing quite a lot of Michael outside of work, aren't you, Kay?' Olive said later as she lay the table in the kitchen with just one place setting.

'There have been a few things going on which aren't particularly pleasant. Michael needs to unwind. I just hope I can help him.'

'He's lucky to have you on his side.'

Kay decided she'd like to confide in Olive and did just that, swearing her to secrecy.

'Tell me about your dealings with Twigge and Moore. I've got the beginning of an idea going around my head.'

Olive looked thoughtful.

'Many years ago I went to them to make my will. That was before they started getting a bad reputation.'

'Would you be prepared to go and see them? You could tell them that the will they are holding isn't valid now, and you're going to make a new one using the services of Harris and Partners. If Charlie is within earshot his reaction might be interesting.'

Having put forward the plan, Kay wondered if she'd done the right thing.

'He is a nasty piece of work, mind. I really don't want you to be involved in anything dangerous.'

Rubbing her hands together, Olive smiled.

'I'm looking forward to it! I used to be in the amateur dramatics group. I'm going to play a vague old woman who doesn't know what she's doing, and see how they treat me. I can't wait!'

* ★ * ★ * ★

Michael and Kay were both quiet during dinner.

'I'm sorry. I'm afraid I haven't been good company.'

'Neither have I,' Kay responded. 'We're both worried about this trouble with Charlie and how it's going to affect the business. He's wants your downfall, Michael. And, after today's meeting, I can't see what we can do about it.'

Michael shrugged.

'I was going to suggest we go dancing, but I don't think either of us feels like it. Why don't we go to that new coffee bar just up the road?'

As they walked in Michael looked round.

'I thought they might all be teenagers in here, but it looks as though I might fit in after all.'

Now that Kay could hear the music pounding from the juke box she did feel like dancing, and was pleased to see a few couples were making use of the small dance space.

Once settled at a black and white, Formica-topped table with their glasses of coffee, Michael seemed to relax.

'This is nice, don't you think?' he asked as he took her hand in his and gave it a tender squeeze. 'And you are absolutely gorgeous. Come on, let's choose some music and dance.'

They quickly agreed on their choice and were soon dancing to the sound of Bill Haley and Jerry Lee Lewis. With such a small, crowded space in which to dance and the extravagant moves necessary to do justice to the music, Kay and Michael found themselves thrown together. After several dances they collapsed together on the bench at their table.

'Not quite your usual type of dancing, is it?'

'I love all dancing,' she said, without adding. 'especially with you.'

'Now you've got colour in your cheeks and your eyes are sparkling. I've been worried about you with all the work and responsibility you've taken on, but you've handled it marvellously. Another coffee?'

'It's time I was getting home. It is Monday, after all.'

She remembered what Vanessa had said about the dinner dance. She wondered who Michael would be taking.

'You're looking thoughtful.'

'It's nothing.'

'Go on, tell me. Something's bothering you.'

'I'm being silly, Michael. Vanessa thought you might ask me to the tennis club dinner dance, and I suppose I wondered if you would. It's just that I'd need to know, in time to shop for something to wear.'

'I'd like to take you more than anybody, but I can't. I've already asked a woman at the tennis club to come with me.'

Kay's heart sank. She'd made a fool of herself.

'Her husband died unexpectedly a few months ago. He was quite a young man. We're all trying to help her in any way we can. Somebody suggested she might like to go to the dinner dance, and I know her quite well, so I thought it would be good to go together. You must know I'd invite you if I could. We really are the best of friends, aren't we?'

'Yes, we are.' She smiled. 'I shouldn't have said anything.'

'I hope you always feel comfortable enough with me to say anything you please. That's what true friendship is all about, that and trust.'

Kay couldn't agree more.

'It was thoughtful of you to invite that woman. How terrible to be in that position — she's so young. Aren't we lucky that we have our health and strength?'

Outside the coffee bar, Michael paused.

'It's a beautiful night. Shall we walk?' He took her hand lightly in his and they sauntered along the road towards Elm

Close where Olive's light was on.

'Would you like to come in for a moment?' she asked.

Michael hesitated then shook his head.

'I'd better get back. We're not all lucky enough to live within a stone's throw of Harris and Partners.'

'I'm still not quite sure where it is you live! I know your parents have a house in the country between Blayton and my parents' home.'

'That's right. I live a few miles from them. You'll have to come and see for yourself one day.'

'I'd like that. Your parents invited me to Sunday lunch one week.'

'I'm glad. They think highly of you, Kay.'

At the front door, Michael let Kay's hand go and dropped a light kiss on her forehead.

'On your own, are you?' Olive called as Kay shut the front door behind her.

'Michael wanted to get home. He's a lot on his mind.'

'Cocoa?'

'No, thanks. We went to the coffee bar and had our drinks in glasses. It was made in a machine and the top was frothy.'

Olive made a face.

'I think I'd rather stick to cocoa.'

The Way to a Man's Heart

The dance class the previous evening had been enjoyable and she'd been pleased to have Len as a dancing partner again. He seemed to enjoy dancing as much as she did. During the break he'd confided to her that he'd been a champion ballroom dancer in his youth. George had been a very particular partner wanting Kay to move in precise ways, but when Kay danced with Len he allowed her a fluidity of motion which enlivened her. It wasn't the same as dancing with Michael, though.

Now she hurried to the shops to get the list Olive had presented her with at breakfast. The butcher gave her a pound of beef skirt and then she called at the greengrocer a few doors along the road where she handed over the list. When he'd packed it all in a bag, she returned home.

'That was quick! I've only just finished washing up.'

'I'm anxious to get going with this stew.' Kay smiled. 'I hope you can bear with me in the kitchen. I did warn you I was hopeless at cooking.'

'You'll be fine. If you write it down as we go along you'll be able to do it on your own another time.'

'Haven't you got a recipe book?'

The kitchen shelf at her parents' home included many cookbooks, but now Kay came to think about it, she'd never seen her mother refer to them when she'd been cooking. She didn't always use the weighing scales either, just a tablespoon or a measuring jug.

'I know this one by heart. It's been my mainstay for a very long time. During the war years, it was mostly vegetables.'

Under Olive's instruction, Kay chopped meat and vegetables and let them simmer away on a low gas.

'It's kind of you to let me invite Michael to eat here this evening. You don't have to go out — he's very taken with you.'

'If only I was ten years younger.' Olive sighed, patting her hair. 'Better make that thirty years! But I'm going to visit the lady next door this evening. She's just come back from a holiday and we'll have a cosy chat about it.'

Kay impatiently lifted the lid of the saucepan, letting loose a wonderful savoury aroma into the kitchen.

'How long does this take?'

'About an hour and a half, and put that lid back on, we don't want it drying out!'

While the stew was cooking, Olive supervised Kay making a trifle.

'It's quite easy when you know how, isn't it?' Kay said, frowning as she put glace cherries on top of the custard. 'The custard was difficult, but that tip about keeping stirring did the trick. You're a good cook, Olive. I envy you.'

'And I envy you your young man. I had a boyfriend many years ago, but not all the men came back from the

Great War. No-one else measured up to anything like him, so I stayed single. I'm very happy and I'm enjoying having you here living with me, Kay.'

'Do you think the stew's done now?' Kay asked, her hand hovering over the saucepan lid.

'Give the meat a test. Stick a knife in and see if it's tender.'

'Like potatoes? I'm happier with vegetables. I sometimes helped Dad dig them from the garden and then cooked them on a Sunday at home.'

'You can do potatoes this evening, then.' Olive peered into the saucepan.

'I wanted to do dumplings, but they'd be as heavy as lead, I'm sure. And they'd be too filling on a day like this. Yes, I'll stick to what I know.'

With the evening meal prepared ahead of time, Kay and Olive made sandwiches for their mid-day meal and then Kay changed into her old clothes and tackled the garden. It was a beautiful afternoon and Olive brought out cups of tea and sat on the seat at the edge of the lawn, watching Kay work.

'Don't wear yourself out,' she called.

'I enjoy it; it's relaxing.'

She found that the physical effort involved took her mind from wandering too much in the direction of Michael. The sun warmed her and she paused in her efforts in order to shrug off her jumper and roll up the sleeves of her blouse. As she picked up the garden fork once more, she saw that Olive had gone from the garden. She remembered that Olive was involving herself in the business of finding out what Charlie Spencer was up to, and she decided to talk seriously with Olive. It was imperative that she didn't endanger herself. Kay knew Charlie was an unscrupulous person, but she hoped he wasn't a dangerous one.

'You're not to worry about me, Kay. I can take care of myself and I'm sure no one's going to harm an old woman in a solicitors' office, are they?'

While Olive laughed, Kay puckered her brow, hoping the older woman was right.

* * *

'I'll be off then,' Olive called to Kay who was in the kitchen making sure things were all in place for the evening. The front door bell rang and Olive opened the door to Michael.

'Hello, Olive. Something smells delicious.'

'It does,' she replied. 'Have an enjoyable time, the two of you, I'm off to see a friend.' She pulled the door shut firmly behind her.

Michael went through to the kitchen where he greeted Kay with a smile and a hug.

'Here's some wine,' he said. 'I wasn't sure what we'd be eating so I brought a bottle of white and a bottle of red.'

'How kind.'

'The white one's already chilled. I put it in my refrigerator at home.'

'As we're having beef, I suppose the red wine is the one to go for.'

As they sipped their wine, Kay suggested they went into the sitting-room.

'Nothing beats home cooking,' Michael remarked.

'Well, I did cook the meal myself, but it was under Olive's instruction. I'm hopeless at domestic chores.'

'Stop putting yourself down, Kay. You do so many things and you do them well.' Michael looked at her. 'Come and sit beside me and tell me a bit more about yourself.'

'You know most of it. The latest thing is the dance competition. I'm really looking forward to that. I hadn't thought of myself as a particularly competitive person, but I hope Len and I win.'

'Len? Is that the new boyfriend?'

'Boyfriend? Where did you get that idea? He's even older than you!' Kay giggled. 'He's the dance instructor and sometimes we dance together.'

She changed the subject.

'I didn't realise Vanessa was engaged. Her fiancé was asleep when I saw him, but I'm sure he's very nice.'

'He is. I think they are getting married at the end of the year. I'm not sure whether or not Vanessa will want to carry on working.'

'What about you?' she managed. 'Have you ever considered getting married?'

Kay watched as he hesitated and colour rose in his cheeks. He cleared his throat before replying.

'Yes, I have.' He looked at Kay and then fixed his gaze on the fireplace. Standing up, he took a sip of wine and paced to the window. 'But I felt the woman in question had been hurt in the past and might not be ready for commitment.'

Why she had asked the question Kay didn't know. She swallowed a lump which had lodged in her throat and forced a smile.

'You're a thoughtful man,' she said.

The silence between them lengthened and Kay knew she ought to change the subject. Hoping she was on a safer footing, she said, 'You're also a very good solicitor. The way you run the office is second to none. Susan and Vanessa agree.'

Michael returned to sit beside Kay.

'So you gossip about me when I'm not around, do you?'

'Of course,' she joked, glad the atmosphere had lightened. 'Isn't that what makes a good employee?'

The repartee continued until Kay remembered the food.

'Please excuse me, I've got to heat the supper.'

Thankful to escape to the kitchen, Kay hurried to put the potatoes on to boil and put a light under the stew. Then she took time to admonish herself. It was nothing to do with her and she must try and put aside her feelings for Michael. They had a whole evening together, however, and Kay was determined to enjoy it.

'This is very good. Cookery can definitely be added to your many attributes.' Michael speared a potato in order to mop up the last smear of juice from his plate.

'Thank you, but I'm not sure you're right. However, I would like to expand my experience as far as work is concerned. I like working for you and taking shorthand notes and typing letters, but it would be exciting to have something a bit more demanding to do.'

'I'm sure I could let you deal with some of the less-complicated work. Under my supervision, of course.'

Kay felt let down. She had hoped he might have thought more of her ability.

'Now, if we can move after that enormous meal, why don't we practise your competition dances? If we push the furniture up to the walls I'm sure there will be room.'

Kay didn't think Olive would mind so long as they put everything back afterwards, so she helped Michael who had already started rearranging the room. She put the radio on.

'Oh, dear, that's not the right sort of music. What can we do?'

'Hum? Sing?'

Kay started humming and Michael quickly joined in. He had a rich, powerful voice. He was also quick to pick up the steps of the two competition dances. He was clearly an amateur, but his enthusiasm made up for his lack of skill.

'What do you think? Am I nearly as good as Len yet?'

'He's been dancing all his life. But you're really very good considering you've only just started. It's been a great help going over the steps with you. Now my only problem is . . . oh, it doesn't matter.'

'Go on, tell me.'

They were standing ready to dance again. Kay was aware of their closeness. He stroked her back gently.

'I need some new shoes for the competition. They're quite expensive and I don't want to ask Mum and Dad for a loan. I shouldn't have told you.'

'When's your birthday?'

'July. Why?'

'I'll buy them for your birthday.'

'You can't possibly do that!' She was shocked.

'I don't see why not. I'd be delighted to. Please let me. We'll go shopping for them one lunchtime next week. Can we get them in Blayton?'

'Yes. Thank you, but I feel awful mentioning for it.'

'Shh.' Michael took her in his arms and pulled her close. Kay was aware of the scent of his body and inhaled deeply. When his mouth met hers she responded in a way she hadn't thought possible. She wound her arms around his neck and gave herself up to the sensation.

'Not watching the television, then?' Olive chuckled as she threw herself down on the settee.

'Oh, I didn't hear you come in, Olive,' Kay said as she and Michael pulled apart quickly.

'That's obvious!'

Michael sat down and chatted to Olive. Kay was in a dream. She had thought she'd loved George, but she could see that hadn't been love. She could really say now she knew what love was.

Dancing Queen

Kay had chosen her lucky dancing shoes with Michael. They were strappy silver sandals with heels higher than she'd dared wear before and made her feel like a princess.

But now she was pleased to be meeting Betty at the bus station. She didn't have long to wait before the bus pulled in. Betty was the first off.

'Hello, Kay, isn't it exciting? I've never been away from home before. What are we going to do? Are we going to your house first?'

Kay laughed.

'So many questions! Let me carry your bag and I'll try and answer them all.'

After a sandwich lunch with Olive, the two young women set off to look round the shops and also to give Betty a tour of the new office.

'Mr Michael's made this ever so nice, hasn't he? Is this your desk? It's so good you're the boss's secretary. You deserve it. Ooh, look at the fridge. Can I open it?'

When Betty was twirling herself round on one of the new office chairs she said, 'I wonder if I did the right thing when I said I wouldn't go out with Charlie. He might be quite nice when you get to know him.'

Kay stopped the spinning and looked Betty in the eye.

'You did absolutely the right thing. There are things I know about Charlie which I can't tell you, but he's no good. You deserve someone much better than him.'

'You deserve someone nice, too, but you haven't got a boyfriend, have you? It doesn't seem right.'

Kay could feel the colour flushing her cheeks. Could she count Michael as her boyfriend or was he still just a friend? Remembering their shared kiss last week she wondered just how he saw her. Since then he'd barely touched her and he hadn't even pecked her on the cheek.

'Mum says my life's all mapped out for me. Marriage and children. I don't know what I want.'

'You're a bright girl. I think you could do very well in your new office. When do you start?'

'A week on Monday. I'm scared, but excited, too. I don't suppose I'll have a friend like you there, but the people I met when I went for my interview seemed nice enough.'

There was a sudden noise.

'What was that?'

'It sounded like glass breaking.'

'Let's go and see.' Kay led Betty back into the kitchen and along a corridor which led to the toilet.

'Who's there?' she called, her voice trembling a little. As they reached the door to the toilet they halted. The sound of feet running along the outside alleyway told them that whoever had been trying to break in had been scared off. Kay pushed the door open. The small window had been broken and glass was strewn across the floor.

'You'll have to tell Mr Michael,' Betty said.

'I'll tell him once I've called the police and arranged for a glazier to come and repair the window.'

'Who do you think it could have been? Was it a thief?'

'I suppose it must have been.' Kay didn't want to voice her suspicions. 'Let me make the phone calls and as soon as the window is fixed I'll take you to a very nice coffee bar Michael and I went to.'

'Mr Michael and you?'

'Yes. We're quite good friends now.'

When Kay arrived home on Monday evening she was exhausted, having had Betty to entertain all weekend. Not that it had been difficult, just that Betty chatted a lot and had wanted to be active all the time. When she saw Michael at the office he had immediately said he thought Charlie would be behind the break-in, but there was no evidence to link him to it. As she was tucking in to a ham salad, Olive spoke.

'I don't want you to be cross with me Kay, but I did what I said I was going to do. I spoke to a Mr Alastair Barnes at Twigge and Moore. I didn't trust him an inch!'

'I've met him, too, and I felt the same.'

'You're a good judge of character. I told Mr Barnes I was re-writing my will and using the services of Harris and Partners. He advised me against such a decision, as there were suggestions in the town that Harris and Partners was not reputable. As I told you, I acted the part of a rather vague old woman, and he did try to bully me. It wasn't a pleasant experience. As I left he was already huddled talking to a man who looked a little weaselly.'

'Charlie! What do you think will happen?'

'I'm not sure. Maybe nothing. Let's

wait and see. It's not big business, is it? An old lady's will.'

'Shall I make you an appointment?'

'An appointment? Oh, I see what you mean. To make my new will. Yes, and I'd like to be seen by Michael, if that's possible.'

Kay hoped that Michael would make sure Olive didn't have to pay the full fee, but deep down she already knew that he would waive the fee completely.

* * *

Every evening Kay practised her dance steps for the competition, and by Saturday she was ready. She left the house early, as Len wanted to have another quick rehearsal. As Kay sat nervously on one of the competitors' seats at the side of the dance floor her attention was taken by a disturbance at the entrance. Michael and Olive were there, laughing and chatting. Olive looked dishevelled.

'Cooee,' Olive called as they headed towards her.

'I'm so pleased to see you both!'

'I wasn't sure I could come. I just turned up on Olive's doorstep.'

'What on earth happened to you, Olive? Your hair!'

'A mess?' Olive patted at her tousled curls. 'I don't care. It was such fun! We came in Michael's car with the hood down. Now, where shall we sit? There are a couple of good seats over there. Good luck, Kay.'

'Yes, good luck.' Michael took her hand and kissed her quickly before following Olive.

Kay and Len took to the floor. Kay was determined to do her very best for the two people who had come to mean so much to her. She let the music wash over her as she lost herself in the moves. Len was an expert and she followed his lead.

When the final note died she knew that she'd danced her best.

'Marvellous,' Len said as he led her

over to their seats.

When all the competitors had performed it was announced that everyone could take to the floor while the judges were reaching their decision. Olive bounced over with Michael following, her bad hip apparently forgotten in her eagerness.

'Well done,' Michael said. 'I know I'm just a beginner, but would you dance with me?'

Kay took his proffered hand. As they were walking away she overheard Olive.

'Don't just sit there, you pudding, let's dance!'

Kay couldn't help but smile when she saw Len propelling Olive round. Her landlady looked to be having the time of her life. Len was the perfect dancing partner and she could already see that Olive was much lighter on her feet than when Kay had last danced with her.

The music stopped and everyone was told to take their seats for the results. Michael relinquished Kay who went and sat next to Len with the other competitors. They gripped each other's hands and waited.

The results were given in reverse order and Kay found herself holding her breath as the pressure increased. A trophy was being handed over to the couple who had achieved the third prize and then the announcer called Kay and Len forward to receive the award for second place.

Although Kay was a little disappointed, she was delighted they'd been placed and, with shining eyes and a big smile, she let Len dance her to the podium. There was tumultuous applause from the audience, urged on no doubt by Michael and Olive, thought Kay as she and Len returned to their seats.

Now all eyes were on the couple in first place. For some reason they didn't appear to be very popular, but Kay clapped hard. It was over.

Michael brought over drinks from the bar and they sat sipping them. Kay felt cross with herself for the discontent she felt. How could she begrudge the winning couple their accolade? Then she heard a voice through the microphone asking for their attention.

'Ladies and gentlemen, it has come to our notice that the winning couple have been disqualified, as they are both on the professional circuit.'

Len put his hand on Kay's and they stared at each other.

'And so,' the announcer continued, 'it gives me great pleasure to announce that Kay and Len are the winners of the competition.'

Michael shook Len's hand and then folded Kay into an embrace, hugging her tightly.

'Well done, you deserve it. Lucky shoes!'

Kay buried her face in Michael's jacket, tears filling her eyes. They'd done it! They'd won! It was what she wanted. But she knew it wasn't all she wanted . . .

Kay and Len shared a taxi to their respective homes and Michael gave Olive a lift back to Elm Close, arriving ahead of Kay. Olive had offered to go in the taxi with Len, but Kay knew she was thrilled to have the opportunity of another ride in the sports car.

On the way home, Len had confided to Kay that he had known about the winners being on the professional circuit. He had challenged them before the competition, but they hadn't backed down. It hadn't been him who had informed the judges, though; it was common knowledge among the regular dancers, and they'd been foolish to think they could get away with it.

As Kay got out of the taxi, Len handed her the first prize cup.

'It'll have to be engraved with our names some time, but until they recall it you keep it.'

Kay was thrilled. She carried it indoors and placed it on the mantelpiece in the sitting room.

Guessing Olive and Michael would be in the kitchen, she went through and found Olive, not heating milk for cocoa, but opening a bottle of whisky.

'Just a small tot to celebrate, Kay. And to help me sleep after all the excitement of this evening.'

Kay declined the offer of the alcohol and Michael had just a polite sip before putting his glass back on the table.

'Len asked to see me again,' Olive said, not looking at Kay or Michael.

'I'm so happy for you. Will you go dancing?'

'Only if someone will buy me a pair of lucky shoes!'

'I don't think you need lucky shoes, Olive,' Michael broke in. 'You and Len seem well suited. When someone special comes along we should grab them with both hands.' He looked across at Kay. 'As long as they are ready, of course.'

Kay was getting mixed messages from him. Sometimes he seemed as though he wanted to be close to her and at others he appeared to be holding back. Maybe he was concerned about their working relationship. It could be awkward if she were to become the boss's girlfriend.

'Well, I'm going to take it as it comes. If we enjoy each other's company it will be a bonus in what has become an exciting life since Kay moved in.' Olive grinned.

'Have there been any more developments regarding Charlie? Kay told me about you seeing Alastair. Have Twigge and Moore been in touch since your visit?'

'No, I haven't heard a dickey bird.'

'I hope it stays that way. I'd better go. Well done, Kay.'

Michael let himself out and the two women sat chatting.

'Len's very nice. I'm glad he wants to see you again.'

'We seem to have a lot in common. He's been involved in amateur dramatics, just like me, so we might both audition for the same production. I wonder if he can cook.'

'He did tell me he likes eating out so I'm sure you'll have some lovely outings.'

'I might have to buy myself a few new

outfits. I haven't been clothes-shopping for a long time. Would you come with me?'

'I'd love to.'

'Good. What a shame your parents couldn't come and see you dance. Still it will be nice for you to show them where you live when they come tomorrow.'

'I'm sure they'll be pleased when they meet you. It will put Mum's mind at rest when she knows I'm in safe hands. And I can ask Dad a few things about the garden!'

A Letter

When she awoke, Kay reached out for her teddy bear and hugged him. Yesterday had been wonderful. Wanting to take another look at the cup on the mantelpiece, she pulled on a light robe and went downstairs. There was no sign of Olive in the kitchen or the sitting room.

Looking out of the back window, she was amazed to see Olive and Len in the garden. She hurried upstairs to wash and dress before going down to join them.

'Len, I'm surprised you're up and about this early!'

'Olive invited me to lunch.' He smiled.

'Is it that time already?' Kay gasped. 'I slept late. I'm sorry, Olive.'

'No need to apologise to me, dear, this is your home now and you can do as you wish.'

'In that case, I'll make a cup of tea. Anyone else like one?'

They shook their heads.

'Len's been looking at the vegetable patch you're digging. He thinks your plans are good.'

Kay enjoyed the praise and spent a few minutes outlining the other ideas she'd had for the garden.

'Sounds ambitious to me,' Len said. 'But you're young and strong and you appear to enjoy a challenge.'

'I'll go and make that tea. Is there anything I can do to help before I go and meet Mum and Dad?'

'I think everything's under control and Len tells me he's good in the kitchen.'

Kay thought they looked as though they'd known each other a long time. They appeared to be so comfortable together. She was pleased for them.

The afternoon with her parents was fun and they arrived back at Olive's shortly before tea time. It wasn't long before Kay's mum was helping Olive in the kitchen and Len and her dad were out in the garden chatting about the war, rationing and the garden. Kay sat on the bench and let it all drift over her.

'Penny for them.'

Kay opened her eyes to see Michael sitting down next to her.

'Hello. Is something wrong?'

'No, Olive asked me to tea. Didn't she tell you?'

She shook her head.

'I'm looking forward to getting to know your parents a bit better. Looks as though Len and your dad are getting on.' He nodded towards the two men who were engrossed in a discussion of what should be planted where. 'Olive and your mum were discussing you and George when I walked in.'

'What were they saying?'

'Your mum said you thought he was the love of your life. Did you?'

'Yes, I did.'

'Hey, you two, come and give us your opinion on this. Harry thinks some fruit bushes should be planted here, and I think they'd be better in this position.'

Kay and Michael looked at each other and laughed.

'I haven't a clue.'

'Me neither.'

'Useless pair,' Len said. He clapped Harry on the back. 'Let's go and see if this tea's ready.'

Kay tried to join in the chatter round the table, but felt slightly unhappy that she hadn't had a chance to explain. If only she had the courage to tell Michael how she felt about him. But she couldn't bear the thought of being rebuffed and then having to look for another job. No, she'd keep quiet and let him think what he liked about her. At least they would remain friends that way.

'I'm so happy that our Kay has found such good lodgings and a lovely landlady. I'll be able to sleep easier.'

'I said she'd be OK. She's well able to look after herself.'

'And she's an excellent secretary,' Michael added.

'Will you all please stop talking about me? Who's going to help me wash up?' Kay started piling up the plates, and her mum was on her feet in seconds.

'It's lovely to see Michael here this afternoon, but I must say I'm surprised. Are you sure there's nothing you want to tell me?' Kay's mother stacked the plates on the worktop.

'Certain, Mum. But perhaps you can tell me why you were discussing me with Olive.'

Her mother coloured.

'It was only about George. We were talking about dancing and, of course, I thought about him. But I'm pleased you won the competition with Len. He's much nicer. I'm sorry, Kay.' She dropped the tea towel and put an arm around her daughter. 'I didn't like to see you so hurt.'

'Shall we forget George?' Kay said.

At that moment, Michael entered the kitchen.

'I came to see if there is anything I can do to help,' he offered, 'but you two seem to have done it all.'

'Kay showed us round this afternoon. You've got a very big office, Michael. I'm sure your hard work will pay off.'

Michael slipped an arm around Kay.

'Any success I have will largely be due to your daughter. She's a wonder; there's nothing she can't handle.'

★　★　★

'Thank you for letting me show my parents around yesterday, Michael,' Kay said when she took the morning's post in to him. 'And I know they enjoyed seeing you.'

'They're nice people and you know I like seeing Olive. She says she has a new lease of life since you came here.'

Kay blushed, wondering what had happened to make Michael so bright and cheerful.

'I'd only have gone to the tennis club if I hadn't visited you. Which reminds me, we should book another game together. We could go this evening, if you like.'

Kay would have loved to accept, but she'd promised Olive she'd watch a nature programme on television with her. Briefly, she thought of inviting Michael to join them, but she couldn't expect him to give up his free time to spend it watching television. He had his own set at home, anyway.

'Can we make it later in the week? I promised Olive that I'd do something with her.'

'You mean she's not seeing Len?' Michael smiled.

'She can't appear too eager,' Kay returned, glad they were getting along so well. Since the previous evening Michael seemed to be in a much lighter mood. She was pleased, but had no idea what had caused it.

'Tomorrow, then?'

Kay looked puzzled.

'Tomorrow what?'

'Tennis. And then we could perhaps go on to that coffee bar again. What do you say?'

'Yes, please. Is it all right for me to

use the club's equipment again, or should I buy a racquet?'

'Might as well use what's there. Perhaps, when you become a member, you can buy your own.'

'Michael, thank you so much for the shoes you bought me. They were lucky for me.'

'You didn't need a pair of lucky shoes to allow you to dance magnificently. That was on your own merit. Which reminds me, I've been thinking about what you said regarding wanting something more demanding to do.'

Kay's attention was caught.

'The other partners and I have come up with an idea. We'd like to offer single ladies a discount if they use our services. We value them as customers, and know they don't earn as much money as men, even when they're doing the same job. Could you come up with something in the way of an advertisement which you think might catch their eye?'

It didn't seem to Kay as if this was a very stimulating thing, but she was happy to be involved.

'Of course. I'll be glad to help you.'

Kay was surprised to get back that evening and find the kitchen empty. She'd been looking forward to telling Olive about her ideas for the advertisement for single women. Olive would be pleased to hear that Michael was looking out for less well paid women who didn't have husbands to support them. Kay wondered if one day things would change and they would be treated equally.

There was no smell of cooking and no sign of Olive. She was alarmed. Ever since she'd moved in Olive had been at home with an evening meal ready and a cheerful greeting. The first thing to do was search the house. She found Olive in the sitting-room clasping a letter. She looked terribly worried and lines etched her face.

'Whatever's the matter?'

'I've had an awful letter.'

'It's from Charlie, isn't it? Well, we knew he'd react to your visit to Twigge and Moore to tell them about removing your business. It was just a matter of time.'

'No, Kay. The letter's from Michael. I can't believe what he's written!' Tears ran down her cheeks.

Kay sat on the arm of the chair and wrapped her arm round Olive.

'May I?' Kay started reading the letter out loud. 'Dear Miss Carter, It has come to our notice that you are not the sort of person we deal with. We expect our clients to be honest and open about their affairs when they instruct us to act on their behalf. Having looked into your account we know that a lot of the property you wish to bequeath after your death is not owned outright by you.'

'It's not true!'

Reading on, Kay gasped, then crumpling the paper she turned to Olive.

'Michael can't have written this, Olive. The man I know wouldn't have written such things. But it is his signature.'

She smoothed out the paper and then read it again, trying to make sense of the letter. It was so unprofessional!

'I'm going to make a cup of tea and bring some biscuits. I don't suppose you've eaten anything all day. Then we'll decide how we're going to deal with this.'

Kay tried to sound stronger than she felt, but standing at the kitchen sink she let the tears fall. She'd loved and trusted George, and he'd let her down badly. Surely Michael wouldn't let her down as well!

The whistling of the kettle brought her back to thinking of Olive and her need to comfort her. Kay carried the tray back into the sitting room and set it down on the little table. She poured tea for them both and made Olive take a biscuit.

'Harris and Partners are doomed to failure,' she said dejectedly.

Suddenly she grabbed the letter and looked at it again.

'Olive, I know who's written this. It

has to be Charlie. Look at the letter heading. It's the old stationery with Harris and Son. We don't use that any more, but that's the paper Charlie stole from the firm to write his reference!'

Olive breathed a sigh of relief.

'I knew it couldn't be Michael. But it was very convincing.'

'Don't blame yourself; I had a moment of doubt, too. I feel awful that I could have thought such a thing. Poor Michael. We'll have to show him the letter and let him decide what to do about it. I'm afraid last time we went to see him Mr Twigge didn't listen to us when we told him about Charlie. But maybe he'd listen if we took this along. I suppose Charlie is just trying to get Harris and Partners into trouble any way he can.'

'It's not like me to be daunted by things, but that was devastating. Not only because I like Michael and trusted him, but also because I know you and he like each other.'

Love, in my case, Kay thought.

There. She'd admitted it, if only to herself. She loved him. It was quite simple.

Once Olive had eaten her biscuit and finished her tea she was back to her usual determined self.

'I've got a plan. We'll have to get Michael's approval and Len's help.'

'Help? Len? What on earth are you talking about?'

'We haven't been in amateur dramatics for nothing. I'm going to cast Len as private investigator Len Hutchings. He'll bring about Charlie's downfall. You just wait and see!'

Guilty!

'I'm not happy about this, Olive.' Michael grimly paced her sitting-room. 'Charlie Spencer is a nasty piece of work. I won't let you put yourself in danger, either of you.'

'Steady on, Michael,' Len put in. 'Olive won't be there, You can come with me if you like — in fact, it would be better if you were there. After all, Miss Olive Carter is a client of yours, isn't she?'

Michael nodded.

'I could come as well,' Kay said, wanting to witness Charlie's disgrace in person.

'No,' both men said in unison.

'You stay at the office, Kay and you stay at home, Olive,' Michael continued. 'We'll be in touch with you both as soon as we've finished with Twigge and Moore.'

The next day Kay went to the office early as between them she and Olive were getting under each other's feet and had only one thing on their minds. Kay desperately hoped she wouldn't have to wait long to hear from Michael and Len that everything had gone smoothly.

Every time the office door opened Kay hoped it would be Michael, but the time passed very slowly and he didn't appear. At last, just before her lunch break, Michael and Len pushed open the door and entered.

'Are you free to come to my office, Kay?' asked Michael, leading the way with Len not far behind him.

Once behind closed doors, Michael invited Kay and Len to make themselves comfortable in the wooden chairs by his desk.

'It's a long story, isn't it Len?' Michael perched on the desk and began. 'Len was very good; in fact, I'm sure he could make a career out of acting.'

Kay grew impatient; she didn't want

to know about Len's theatrical ability at the moment. All she was interested in was whether Charlie had got his comeuppance.

'Michael did well, too. He didn't interrupt while I was giving Charlie a warning, even though I could see he was itching to,' Len added.

'Will you please just tell me what happened!'

'Len and I asked to see Charlie Spencer. As luck would have it, Mr Twigge was in the outer office and let us have his room for our interview. He came into the room with us and said he would act as Charlie's witness in case he was being put under undue pressure. Len said he was a private detective acting on behalf of a client. You should have seen Charlie's face! Guilt was written all over it.'

Michael grinned.

'Len outlined what was written in it, making sure Olive's name wasn't mentioned. Then he said he had reason to believe Mr Spencer was behind the duplicity. Both Charlie and Mr Twigge asked for proof, and I thought we were lost, but then Charlie went beetroot red and said it couldn't have been him as he hadn't had any direct dealings with Miss Carter. Of course he realised straight away that he'd put his foot in it by mentioning Olive's name. And so did Mr Twigge.'

'So he dug a hole for himself?'

'Correct! Suffice it to say that Mr Twigge will deal with Charlie Spencer. He was as outraged as we were when he realised what Charlie had been up to. And then, as if that wasn't enough, Charlie said it wasn't just him — Alastair Barnes was involved as well. It seemed the pair of them wanted to discredit both us and Twigge and Moore so that they could set up an office together, here in Blayton.'

'What will happen to the two of them?'

'I don't know, but I am sure that neither of them will work in any law firm ever again.'

The three of them sat in silence until Kay spoke.

'Does Olive know? We must tell her at once. She'll be a nervous wreck by now, wondering how it all went.'

Len was on his feet.

'I'll go.' He grinned. 'She'll want to see my disguise.'

Kay hadn't noticed, but now she looked closely at Len she could see he had different spectacles on, and it looked as if he'd grown a moustache overnight. And in spite of the warmth of the day, he was wearing a mackintosh with the belt tied tightly around his middle. He did look every inch a detective!

Left together, Kay and Michael exchanged a look.

'I'm so pleased this has all been sorted out.' Kay sighed. 'I was worried we — that is, the firm — would get a bad reputation based on the false rumours.'

Michael took her hand.

'Thank you for your concern, my

dear Kay. We can put all that behind us and concentrate on being the best solicitors' office in Blayton.'

'I thought we were already!' She squeezed his hand.

'You know, I thought Twigge was implicated in some way, but after seeing how he reacted to Charlie's confession this morning, I'm sure he didn't know a thing about it. I think we could become close business associates. Your instinct about Alastair was very intuitive.'

Basking in the praise, Kay wanted to tell him about the advertisement she had drafted, but now was not the time.

'We'll have to go out and celebrate this evening.'

'I think Len and Olive may have other plans.'

'I wasn't asking them out, just you.' He brought Kay's hand to his lips and tenderly kissed it. 'But I've just had a thought. It's Friday. Won't you be going to your dancing class?'

'It won't matter if I miss one class. But why don't we see if there's a band playing at the Orchid Ballroom?'

'Dinner first, then dancing. Perfect!'

★   ★   ★

Kay had worked slightly later than six so didn't have long to get ready before Michael called for her. Olive and Len were just finishing off their meal when Kay walked into the kitchen.

'Hello, dear. I hope you don't mind, but Len's been doing a bit of work in the garden. He's not interfering.'

'I'm happy to have help. Thanks, Len.'

'My pleasure. I've been rewarded with a magnificent meal. I'm not sure about dancing well tonight, Kay, not after eating all the food Olive's provided.'

'I'm not coming this evening, I'm going out with Michael. I didn't think you'd mind me missing this once. You're still going to the class, though, Olive?'

Olive nodded vigorously, a wide grin on her face.

219

'I'll be back again next week. We're going to start work on the dances for that next competition, aren't we?'

'We certainly are. We must get some other members of the class to enter as well. Some of them are very good, and could be placed if they worked hard enough.'

As Kay went upstairs to get ready she thought how lucky she was. She had really come up trumps when she'd found Olive to lodge with and now with dancing, the garden and her ever deeper involvement at work she had plenty to enjoy.

And then there was Michael. A deep thrill ran through her as she pictured him sitting at his desk concentrating, his hair flopping forward over his piercing blue eyes.

She didn't have time to daydream, but in spite of that she lay on the bed and went back over their outings together, the times he'd taken her in his arms and the times they'd kissed. She knew she had to be patient and wait and see how things went between them. He hadn't ever said he loved her, but then she hadn't told him her feelings. Should she, or would that spoil their relationship?

No, she decided, getting up off the bed and starting to get ready, she would let things take their course. If their relationship didn't develop any further then she would have to live with it. But for now she would make the most of the opportunity to spend time with Michael. And the most pressing problem at the moment was what she should wear!

'You look lovely, Kay.' Michael took her arm and led her into the restaurant. 'I hope you like it here. It's only just opened. In fact, I drew up the papers for the new owners.'

'I think you fit into the town very well.' Kay looked around the room. 'There are quite a few people here even though it's early. I hope it turns out to be popular. When someone's put a lot of effort into something it's nice to see them rewarded.'

Michael smiled, taking a proffered menu from a waiter.

'Let's see if their food warrants it. I'm starving. And at least we can put the worry of Charlie Spencer behind us now. That's the reason for us being here this evening. To celebrate that.' Michael lifted a glass of wine which the sommelier had poured. 'I think we should dedicate this toast to Mr Twigge.'

Kay was disappointed. She had hoped for something more personal between them, but even now Michael was still thinking about work.

'I think we should toast Olive and Len,' she protested. 'They did far more than Mr Twigge in getting to the bottom of Charlie's deception.' She felt irritation rising in her.

Quickly Michael replaced his drink on the table and covered Kay's hand with his.

'I've upset you. I'm sorry. I can be so clumsy at times.'

'You always seem preoccupied with work,' Kay couldn't help bursting out. 'Even when you're . . . '

Michael looked at her quizzically.

'When I'm what?'

She'd been about to add 'with me', but had realised how forward that would have been.

'Even when you're supposed to be relaxing after a hard day at work.' Changing the subject, she said, 'By the way, I wanted to let you know that I've handed in an advertisement at the Labour Exchange.'

'Why? You don't mean you're looking for another job, do you? Kay, I can't manage without you!'

Mollified slightly by the fact that Michael appreciated her — in a work situation at least — Kay smiled.

'Of course I'm not looking for another job. I was referring to the assignment you gave me to give single ladies a discount. Do you remember?'

He loosened his grip.

'Of course. Thank you, but why the

Labour Exchange?'

'Because that's where people go to get jobs, and there will be a lot of single ladies passing through. I know someone who works there and she said they'd display the notice.

'She also said it was a very welcome idea, and that she might make an appointment herself to see you next week. I think a lot of women have problems knowing where to turn to for help and guidance when it comes to the legal aspects of renting property, employment and so on.'

'I'll be very happy to help, if I can. And if not, perhaps I can advise as to where they can get the assistance they need. I've been so lucky in my career, Kay, that I feel I must do something in return.'

The food was delicious and Michael sent their compliments to the chef before they left to go to the Orchid Ballroom.

'I'm not sure if I should be dancing with you,' Michael said as they found chairs at a vacant table in the ballroom. 'You being a prize-winning dancer!'

Kay laughed.

'You're coming along quite nicely.'

'Only 'quite nicely'? That doesn't sound promising.' He frowned. 'I'll have to put more effort in, I can see.'

The evening went well and Kay relaxed as usual when she moved to the music. Michael wasn't as instinctive a dancer as Len, but she felt good in his arms.

During a break in the music, Kay waved to a few people she'd got to know about the town.

'You know a lot of people, Kay.'

She shrugged.

'I go up and down the high street quite a lot. You know, to and from work and to the post office and, of course, shopping. I see people.'

'Perhaps, if I didn't use the car as much, I'd mingle more with the locals.'

'Olive and I are going shopping tomorrow. Now she's seeing Len she wants some new clothes. It's lovely for her to have a new companion and new interests.'

'It must be lovely for her to have you as a friend,' Michael replied.

Key of the Door

'I've never seen such an array of clothes!' Olive moved the garments along the rail in the department store.

'When did you last come in here?'

'I can't remember. My clothes don't seem to wear out now I'm a bit older. When you're young it's nice to have different dresses and coats, but I've never had occasions to wear elegant things to.'

'Now you have. Where's Len taking you next week?'

'All he said was that we were going out to eat.'

She took a pretty yellow dress and held it up against her.

Kay shook her head.

'You'll look like a daffodil in that. Something a bit more subtle, I think. How about this one?'

She held up an aquamarine jacket with a peplum.

'This is a bit like the one the Queen wore in Australia. We saw it on a newsreel on the television, do you remember?'

'She's a lot younger than I am,' Olive said doubtfully, looking at the pretty garment. 'I think it's going to be a bit too constraining.'

Kay replaced it and pulled out a flowery print dress with a dropped waist and a boat neck.

'I like that. Is it my size? Let's see what it looks like on.'

'You look lovely!' Kay said as Olive stood in front of the fitting-room mirror.

'Yes, madam, I agree with your daughter,' the shop assistant said. 'It really suits you.'

Kay and Olive smiled at each other. Olive added a skirt and blouse plus a light cardigan to her pile on the counter.

'Are you buying anything, Kay?'

'I like this jacket. It's a pretty colour, but I'm not sure about it.'

Her hand stopped along the rail and she extracted an attractive dress which was white with red polka dots. It had a V-neck, fitted bodice and full skirt.

When she tried it on, it was as if it was made for her. She felt wonderful in it and she hoped she'd have an occasion to wear it very soon.

Olive asked the assistant if they could leave their purchases behind the counter while she and Kay went to the cafeteria for a cup of tea.

Once there they sank into chairs and gave the waitress an order for tea and scones.

'I'm so pleased you and Len are friendly,' Kay said before taking an enormous bite of buttered scone.

'I feel I've known him all my life. I'm just so comfortable with him.' Olive poured the tea into their cups. 'And you and Michael?'

'Oh, you know, just the same. I'm still not sure where I am with him. I'm pleased that business with Charlie is out of the way and he can concentrate on his work.'

Then she admitted, 'To be truthful, I wish he'd concentrate on me rather than on his work!'

She giggled to make a joke out of it, but she was serious about what she'd said.

As her birthday approached Kay waited to see if Michael or Olive would make any suggestions for her twenty-first. It was a work day so she would visit her parents for a birthday tea the following weekend.

She'd hung the polka dot dress on the door of her wardrobe so that she could admire it, and thought it would be perfect for a birthday outing with Olive, Len and Michael.

But time passed and there was no sign of an invitation. Michael was preoccupied at work, and although they saw each other every day their social life together had waned completely.

* * *

'Morning, dear,' Olive said, as she placed a plate of tomatoes on toast in front of Kay.

'That looks good. What are you up to today?'

'Nothing much. Just the usual. You'd better get a move on. Look at the time.' Olive nodded towards the clock.

Having wolfed down her breakfast Kay headed for the office. If there were any birthday cards for her they would arrive whilst she was at work.

Michael was already in the office engrossed in a pile of paperwork.

'Hello, Kay. Could you fetch me the Davidson file, please?' There were dark circles under his eyes and he was unshaven. It was unlike him to be anything other than perfectly groomed and Kay was immediately alarmed.

'What's wrong?'

'Nothing to concern you.'

Kay felt hurt.

'Michael, we're friends aren't we? If

something's bothering you, don't you think you should share it with me? I might be able to help.'

'It's not very likely. But I suppose it's time I told you what's been going on. You're right, it will be a relief to tell you. Just before I left work yesterday evening the bank rang and confirmed my suspicions.'

'What is it? What's happened?'

'Charlie.'

'I thought he'd confessed, and that was the end of all your difficulties with him.'

'No. It seems that the Charlies of this world never give up. As you know, we decided not to press charges as Mr Twigge said he'd deal with Charlie and Alastair. But it turns out Charlie has a friend who works at the local bank, our bank.

'There have been dubious goings-on, and the bank manager has discovered discrepancies in the paperwork. One consolation is that we are not the only local business to have been involved, so it's likely that Charlie and Alastair will get their just deserts.'

'How come nobody noticed sooner? Surely there must have been constant checking of the accounts?'

'It's happened over quite a short time and they used the opportunity of a change in bank manager to commit their crime. If you remember, the old manager retired and the new one has only just been appointed. Charlie's clever. He's seen his chance and taken it.'

'What happens now?'

'I'm not sure, Kay. With the expansion the future looked promising, but now . . . I just don't know.'

Kay longed to take him in her arms and comfort him.

'It's not the end of everything. I'm sure we can all pull together, even take pay cuts if necessary. Your staff are very loyal and will support you in whatever way they can.'

'I knew they would, but this is such a blow after all our hard work setting up the office here in Blayton. I'm not even sure how it will affect me personally. Maybe I'll have to sell my car and house.'

'It doesn't matter, does it? It's the people in our lives who are important, not things.'

Michael patted her hand.

'I wish I'd told you sooner. It's as though a weight has been lifted off my shoulders.'

'Do you know what I think you should do? Go home, have a relaxing bath, shave and put on some fresh clothes. We can manage very well without you this morning.'

'I think I will. Come with me, please. We can have some lunch and come back here this afternoon. The break will do us both good.'

Michael's home was modest and just how Kay imagined a bachelor's home would be. After Michael had made them both a cup of tea he took his upstairs leaving her with a pile of magazines.

She wandered into the kitchen to see

what they might have for lunch and decided on eggs as there wasn't much else in the pantry or fridge. By the time Michael appeared she'd laid the table and had sliced the bread and beaten the eggs ready to cook.

'This looks good.' Michael towelled his still damp hair and sat down at the table.

The scrambled eggs on toast were soon devoured and Michael looked at his watch.

'Would you like to see the garden while you're here?'

'As long as we're not late back at the office.'

'We've plenty of time. I'm the boss, after all.' His face fell. 'For the time being, at least.'

They wandered outside.

'These smell beautiful.' Kay inhaled the aroma of a mature rose and caressed its velvety petals.

'So do you.' He put an arm around her shoulders and pulled her to him.

They sat together on the grass and

listened to the bees buzzing in and out of the flowers and the birds singing. It was so peaceful and Kay wanted to stay there for ever.

Too soon, he held out his hand and pulled her to her feet.

'Time to go, I'm afraid. Back to the grindstone.'

'Wasn't that Olive?' Kay cried as Michael drove slowly along the high street to the office.

'I don't think so,' he replied. He placed a hand on her arm and pressed it, almost forcing her, it seemed, to turn and look at him.

Kay preceded Michael into the office and gasped. The reception area was festooned with brightly coloured balloons and there was a hand-made banner proclaiming: *Happy Birthday, Kay.*

Tears of happiness pricked her eyes. How could she think she'd been forgotten?

She caught sight of Michael grinning and yes, there was Olive. So it had been her!

'Thank you all very much.' It was all Kay trusted herself to say without making a fool of herself.

'Here you are, dear. I've brought the cards from the first and second post.' Olive handed over a stack of envelopes.

In the middle of the reception desk was an iced cake with Kay's name on it and twenty-one candles.

'See if you can blow them out in one go.'

It took three attempts before Kay managed to extinguish them all and everyone clapped when she'd accomplished it.

Afterwards, Vanessa and Olive cleared up the office while Kay followed Michael to his room. 'I hope you didn't think we'd forgotten your birthday. We wanted to make it a surprise for you.' At that moment the phone on Michael's desk rang. He answered it and held out the receiver to Kay. 'It's for you.'

'Kay Watson speaking. Oh, Mum, what a surprise to hear you. Thank you for my pretty card.' She chatted some more and then replaced the handset. 'I expect you arranged that as well, did you?'

Michael nodded.

'And I'd like to suggest one more thing to add to your day. Would you come out with me this evening?'

'As long as it's not to eat, I'd love to.' Kay giggled.

★ ★ ★

It was a treat for Kay to be in the Odeon in Blayton. She sat close to Michael and they laughed their way through 'Carry On Sergeant', enjoying the performances of Kenneth Williams and Charles Hawtrey.

'Olive and Len would enjoy this,' she whispered.

It was good to hear Michael hooting with laughter and even better to feel her hand in his. When the lights went up she felt a tap on her shoulder. It was George.

'Happy birthday! I never forgot, did

I, Kay? Over the years you had some lovely cards and gifts from me, didn't you? And you're twenty-one today. Got the key of the door. Hope you don't mind if I have a word with Kay,' he said to Michael, who immediately stood up.

'I'll see you in the foyer when you're ready.' Michael strode off without even waiting for the National Anthem to finish.

'What do you want?'

'I wondered if you'd go out for a meal with me later in the week. I'll take you to that posh place that's just opened. I need to talk to you about our future, dancing and all the rest of it. I thought we could discuss practising for some competitions.'

'Really?'

'I knew you'd be pleased. When I saw you here on your twenty-first birthday, it felt as though fate had a hand in us getting together again. I know I broke your heart and I'm sorry. I want to make it up to you. I always loved you, you know. Please forgive me.'

At one time Kay's heart would have melted at his plea, but now it was as hard as ice.

'You've got things all wrong, George. I've got a wonderful new dancing partner and a lovely new boyfriend. I'm having the time of my life and I don't need you in it. Remember how you deserted me for your new girlfriend? Well, I'm sorry if it didn't work out for you, but I'm sure you'll meet your soul mate one day. Now, if you'll excuse me I want to join my boyfriend.'

Kay's heart was racing as she joined Michael in the foyer.

'Are you all right?'

'I'm absolutely fine and I'd very much like to go to the coffee bar to dance. What do you say?'

'Yes. It's your special day and we'll do whatever you want.'

Kay linked her arm through his and as they walked out of the building she spotted George flirting with a group of girls. It hadn't taken him long to get over her rebuttal. She didn't know what she'd ever seen in him!

Olive wasn't up when she got in as it was nearly midnight so she quickly got ready for bed. Sleep wouldn't come. After the initial disappointing start she'd had the most wonderful day, and Michael had surprised her with another small gift at the coffee bar.

He'd handed her a small box tied with ribbon and inside was a delicate silver chain with a silver rose with K and M entwined. He had taken it and gently put it round her neck before doing up the clasp.

She touched it now, as she hadn't wanted to take it off. She'd chosen the shoes herself, but Michael had chosen the necklace, making it an exceptional gift. She would treasure it for the rest of her life, however her relationship with Michael went.

Lying in the dark, though, Kay knew that if things didn't work out for them then her heart really would break.

Rescue

'Good day, then, yesterday, dear?' Olive asked as she poached eggs for their breakfast.

'Wonderful. I've got so much to tell you. Let's have an evening in together and a good chat. I'll cook.'

'That would be lovely, but I don't know if I can wait to tell you my bit of news.' Olive put the plates on the table and sat down.

'Go on, then, tell me.'

'I'm afraid you'll be shocked. It's quite out of character. I'm a great planner, but sometimes you have to grab what's offered with both hands. We're not getting any younger. I mean Len and me.'

'I've no idea what you're talking about.'

'Len came round yesterday evening.'

'That's all right. You don't need a chaperone!'

'We had a meal, listened to the radio and then we talked. I noticed he was a bit edgy and eventually he asked me something rather exciting.'

'I'll guess. You're going on holiday.'

Olive giggled.

'Yes, we will be having a holiday together. We'll definitely do that, but I'm not having a honeymoon without first getting married.'

'You're getting married?' Kay was shocked. 'But you hardly know each other.'

'We feel as though we've known each other all our lives. I know people will react badly, and possibly think I'm silly to accept so soon, but it feels completely right. We love each other. It's that simple.'

'That's a big surprise, but it's wonderful news, Olive. If you're both sure, then I wish you every joy. Len's a lovely man and I think you'll be happy together. When's the big day?'

'We thought a September wedding would be nice. We don't want to wait long. It won't be a big do, but I want it to be perfect. I'll need your help with choosing the dress, deciding on food, with everything, really.'

'I'll be delighted. We can start planning this evening. How exciting, I can't believe it.'

'Neither can I. I didn't think I'd ever have this much happiness after I lost my boyfriend in the war. It's you, you know. You've brought sunshine into my life.'

Kay skipped to work. She couldn't wait to tell Michael the news. In fact she told everyone in the office and some of the clients. She just couldn't keep it to herself.

* * *

'What on earth have you got in there?' Kay's mum asked, taking the heavy case from her daughter at the front door.

'I thought I'd bring some clothes home and swap them for a few dresses which are still in the wardrobe. It's so warm now.' Kay hugged her mother and walked into the house. 'Where's Dad?'

'Where do you think?'

Kay let herself out of the back door. As she headed towards the vegetable patch, she could see her father's bent figure.

He looked up and smiled letting go of the garden fork he was wielding.

'It's good to see you. Thanks for coming home. Your mother is really pleased.'

Together they picked a few peas and selected some salad vegetables before going into the house.

'As you weren't here for your birthday, Kay, we've saved your present for now.'

Mrs Watson pointed to a large rectangular parcel in the middle of the sitting room.

'Go on, open it.'

Tearing eagerly at the wrapping paper, Kay couldn't think what on earth would be inside. Whatever it was would be a surprise. Her birthday seemed to be going on for a very long time.

With shining eyes, she looked up at her parents as she kneeled on the floor.

'A gramophone!' she cried. 'Why, it's just what I want and need. I'll be able to practise my dancing at Olive's now. Thank you, Mum, thank you, Dad!'

'We wanted to buy a couple of records to go with it,' her father said, 'but we don't know what you young people like these days. So, here, take this money and buy them yourself.'

'That's too much,' Kay protested. 'You spoil me.'

'Talking of dancing,' her mother said, 'there is another card here which we didn't forward to you.'

She shot a glance at her husband.

'We think it's George's handwriting and we didn't know if you'd want to receive it. We didn't want to upset you. I know you said he meant nothing to you, but it's not always good to drag up the past.'

Taking the envelope, Kay slit it open and looked at the card with its flowery picture and message.

It was from George, and he'd signed it *with love.*

Whatever was George thinking? She hoped that since their talk at the Odeon he would have got the message by now.

Sighing, she put it on the mantelpiece and returned her attention to the record player. Experimentally she turned the handle on the side of the machine and then inspected the needle attached to the arm.

'There's a little box with some spare needles in, see?'

Her father crouched beside her.

'I wish we had a record we could try it out with.'

'I thought I'd go into town this afternoon, and call on Betty on the way. Is that all right? I don't want to desert you, but it would be nice to see her and the old place.'

'You'll see that Harris and Son has closed down now. It looks a bit forlorn, the empty building. How are things in Blayton, Kay? Let's have lunch and you can let us know all the news.'

Not sure what to tell her parents about Michael, Kay just said that the business was growing and then she told them about Olive and Len.

'I'm so pleased,' her mother said. 'Olive's a really nice person.'

Her father looked serious.

'Where does that leave you, then, Kay?'

Pausing, her fork halfway to her mouth, Kay said, 'What do you mean? I don't understand.'

'After the wedding, where will they live? If Len moves into Olive's house they won't want a lodger, I wouldn't imagine. And if Olive moves in with Len, I suppose her house will go up for sale.'

The enjoyment of the meal was taken away. Kay toyed with her food, unable to fully appreciate the tinned fruit salad and evaporated milk which was a favourite in summertime in the Watson household.

With her suitcase in her old familiar bedroom, Kay unpacked it and hung up the clothes she'd brought home. She'd wait until tomorrow to choose what she wanted to take back.

If she had the heavy gramophone to carry she wasn't sure what else she could manage.

Changing her blouse, she went back downstairs and left the house to tour the town she knew like the back of her hand.

* * *

'Betty, I was hoping I'd see you! In fact I was going to call on you.'

The two friends had met as they were window-shopping, by chance.

'Thank you for my birthday card. The office gave me a surprise party and Mum phoned me at work to wish me a happy birthday.'

They brought each other up to date with news and Kay was delighted that Betty was doing well in her new job.

'I'm doing more than I was with Harris and Son, and now I'm in charge of the duplicator. Remember you showed me how to work it? I owe you such a lot, Kay.'

Her face reddened.

'And I'm dating a young man. He must be nice because even my mum likes him.'

Kay beamed at her friend.

'We'll have a cup of tea to celebrate after I've done a bit of shopping.'

After having fun buying a record, Kay nipped into the sweet shop to get a quarter of humbugs for Olive. Then the pair went to a café for tea and a sticky bun.

Her problems were forgotten, for the time being at least, and Kay found her appetite had returned.

'How's Mr Michael? Tell me about the others in the office. I sometimes see Susan at weekends when she comes back home, but we were never close, not like you and me.'

Kay went on to tell Betty about the

goings on in Blayton. She felt she should mention Charlie Spencer in case there was an item of news in the local paper.

'But what about you and Mr Michael,' Betty persisted. 'I'd have thought you'd be engaged by now!'

Choking on the last dregs of her tea, Kay tried to pass the remark off as a light-hearted joke. But to her it was no laughing matter.

Her dad walked her to the bus stop carrying the gramophone. Kay had decided not to attempt to take the suitcase back with her. She'd have to collect some more clothes on another visit.

'I've had a lovely time this weekend. And you've been really generous to give me such a wonderful present. Thanks for everything, Dad. Don't worry about waiting with me for the bus, it's bound to turn up. I know you've got some things you want to do in the garden.'

Kay couldn't wait to show Olive her present, but at the back of her mind was the worry about losing her room when Len and Olive married.

She felt she'd never find another place where she felt so at home and she'd never find another landlady quite like Olive.

Just when she was feeling settled, and things were working out for her, everything had to start going wrong! But she wouldn't ever begrudge Olive and Len their happiness.

'Well, look who it is.'

She suspected George had been drinking again.

'Hello, George, how are you?'

'How do you think I am? My girlfriend left me and you won't go out with me, even though you're in love with me.'

'I'm not.'

'That's not what you said when we parted.'

'That was a long time ago and things have changed since then. Please just leave me alone.'

'Kay?'

Michael had pulled up at the bus stop. He jumped out of the car and she felt a stab of joy at seeing him. She had been a bit frightened as to what George would do.

Michael reached down to pick up her parcel.

'Is this yours? Come on, I'll give you a lift back to Olive's.'

'Yes, please.' Kay was relieved to have escaped from George. She hoped she wouldn't ever encounter him again.

'Did you have a good time?'

'Lovely. Mum and Dad bought me a gramophone. That's what's in the parcel.'

'That's wonderful. The four of us will be able to dance at Olive's!'

'I'm not so sure. Dad made me realise that Olive and Len maybe won't want me living with them. I was so pleased for them I hadn't thought about my situation.'

'That's typical of you, not to think of yourself. That's one of the things I lo — That is, I'm sure things will be fine.'

Kay didn't think he sounded certain and she sat quietly for the rest of the journey.

★   ★   ★

'Isn't it wonderful, Olive?' Michael asked as he danced her round the sitting-room.

'Marvellous. We'll have a lot of fun. Len and I will get a few records next time we're out shopping together. I fancy some Bing Crosby. Kay, you're very quiet. You have been ever since you got in.'

'It's nothing, really.'

'Go on, tell Olive your concerns about when she and Len get married.' Michael nodded.

'It's just something Dad said when I was at home. You'll be moving in with Len, or Len will move in here. Either way, you won't want me about.'

'Don't be so silly, of course we want you to stay! It's all settled. We've discussed and decided everything. Len is selling his place and moving in here. There's plenty of room and you can stay as long as you like.'

Kay was relieved. She turned to Michael.

'Did you see who was at the bus stop? It was George. He was quite horrible. I was very pleased when you turned up.'

'Good,' Michael said as he started the gramophone again. 'Would you like to dance?'

After Michael had left, Kay and Olive listened to the music again as they chatted about the wedding. Kay made lists of everything that needed doing.

'We've seen the vicar and he can slot us in during September. I've decided to have the reception here. There won't be many of us and I think it will be friendlier than a hotel room. I will prepare most of the food and people can help themselves. Thank goodness rationing is over.'

'I'd like to help with the food, if you'll let me.'

'I was hoping you'd volunteer. I also wondered if you'd be my bridesmaid. Not exactly a bridesmaid, but if you'll just be there, to help me out with things.'

'Who's going to give you away?'

'I hadn't thought of that! Maybe you would. You could give me away and then do things like hold my bouquet. You're very good at doing more than one job at once.'

'I'm honoured that you've asked me, Olive. I'd love to do whatever I can to make this the best day of your life.'

*   *   *

Later that week Michael was in a very good mood after receiving a phone call put through by Vanessa.

'Kay,' he called, 'please come through.'

Wondering what was happening, Kay hurriedly picked up her notebook and pencil and went to Michael's room.

'Good news,' he said, closing the

door behind her. 'Sit down and I'll tell you all about it.'

'Oh,' Kay began. 'Your father phoned earlier today.'

Michael was immediately alert.

'I didn't get that message. Don't tell me Vanessa didn't put it through?'

'Actually, the call was for me. He's invited me to eat with them on Sunday.'

'That's good news. He said he would. Let me give you a lift. I'll be going there as well.'

Kay had hoped he would be, and a lift would be a great help as she had no idea exactly where Mr and Mrs Harris lived!

She made herself comfortable, pleased to see that Michael's despair during office hours lately had dispelled.

'That was Mr Twigge on the telephone. Between us we've managed to sort things out at the bank. Spencer and Barnes won't cause any more trouble.'

'I'm relieved about that,' Kay said. 'But I've a feeling there's something else on your mind.'

Michael smiled.

'You know me well, don't you? And you're right. Mr Twigge has asked if we'll take over a couple of large accounts from his firm, as he's inundated with business. I can't understand why he suggested that out of the blue. I've accepted, and would be pleased if you could help me out.'

Kay felt the colour rise in her cheeks.

'I suppose I'd better confess. I went to see Mr Twigge to make the suggestion. It seemed silly that he had too much work to keep on top of things and we needed more.'

'You're a marvel.'

'I'd love to help you out. It's just what I want. Thank you. It'll be a challenge, but I'm sure I'm up to it. I've been a bit preoccupied with Olive and Len's plans lately, but I promise to devote myself to you from now on.'

Realising what she'd said, her hand went to her mouth.

'To the firm, I mean.'

'That's a pity,' Michael replied, bending and brushing her mouth with his lips. 'I'd like you to devote yourself to me.'

The ringing telephone brought them both back to earth.

Heart to Heart

Kay was very happy and enjoying the drive. It was a beautiful sunny day and the countryside was looking pretty with its rolling hills and wooded areas.

She couldn't help but wish she was just going out with Michael, as she was nervous about spending time with his parents. She knew they had a large house and lived a different sort of life from her own family.

To help her confidence, Kay was wearing her new polka dot dress, and hoped she would be acceptable.

'You're very quiet this morning,' Michael said, glancing at her. 'Is something wrong?'

'No, nothing.' As soon as she said it she realised that she should be honest with him. 'That's not true. Olive told me I shouldn't worry, just be myself, but I'm anxious about visiting your parents.

'I've only met them at office functions or in relation to work. I find it quite daunting. I won't know what to say, and I probably won't know which cutlery to use for what.'

He laughed.

'Don't worry. Dad doesn't mind about that sort of thing and he always gets it wrong. Honestly, Kay, my parents are very relaxed. They're not ogres waiting to jump at the chance of criticising you. Why would they?'

She didn't answer. Nor could she understand why she'd been invited in the first place.

'Will anyone else from the office be there? The partners, Vanessa or anyone else?'

'No, it's just you, as far as I know.'

That increased the pressure, but it turned out he was absolutely right about his parents being relaxed. Although the house was much grander than she was used to, she soon felt comfortable and the meal went well with lots of chatting about the office, tennis and dancing.

It came as a surprise to Kay that Mrs Harris had cooked the Sunday roast herself. Somehow she'd imagined they'd have a cook and a housekeeper, but they appeared to be just a normal couple who lived in a big house.

When Kay mentioned that she was interested in gardening Mrs Harris insisted they go for a stroll round their garden, as she wanted help with plans for a new flower bed. It was quite different from Olive's bare garden and Michael's functional one, but very lovely.

'Now that you've seen the garden, let's sit on the bench by the pond and enjoy the sunshine. It's nice to have female company for a change. I expect Robert and Michael will be discussing business, as usual. It's been a very important part of Robert's life, and Michael takes it all very seriously. I do wonder how Robert will manage his spare time, when he lets go of the reins completely.'

'I have noticed that Michael puts work first.'

'That was very heartfelt, Kay. I must tell you that we are very happy that Michael and you are going out.'

'But . . . '

'He hasn't ever told us much about his past girlfriends, but your name is for ever popping up. He is always saying how wonderful you are. I shouldn't say this, but I've been quite lonely at times. I wasn't able to have a career. It was expected that I would stay at home and look after the family and with Robert working such long hours I spent a lot of time alone.'

She sighed.

'I had friends, of course, but it wasn't the same as having my husband at home. Things are changing, and Michael is different from his father. I think that once he has got things going in Blayton he will be perfectly happy to let the new partners take a large role in the business. He will be able to spend time with his family — when he has one.'

Michael came towards them pushing a wheelbarrow.

'Are you two all right? You look very serious.'

'We've been having a nice chat, and it wasn't all about you, so don't think it was.' Michael's mother smiled at him.

'I'll go and check on your father. I'll make some lemonade and bring it out later.'

'I'll come and help with the digging,' Kay said, following Michael.

'No, you won't. I don't want to be responsible for you getting your dress mucky. You can continue to look beautiful, making daisy chains.'

I'd rather watch you, Kay thought to herself. Michael rolled up the sleeves of his shirt and set to work.

They didn't talk much. Kay listened to the bees humming and the birds singing in the trees. Kay watched his strong muscles working as he dug the soil.

Mrs Harris brought out the lemonade and Michael stopped briefly to gulp it down.

Kay couldn't think of a better way to spend a sunny Sunday afternoon. Here she was in a beautiful garden with the man she loved.

'There, I've finished.' Michael thrust the spade into the ground. 'What do you think?'

'It's a wonderful bit of digging, the best ever, I'm sure.'

'Flattering the boss?'

They both laughed, but then it struck Kay that the problem with their relationship might be that she was his secretary. With a heavy heart Kay realised what she must do. If she and Michael were going to have a chance of a future together she would have to look for another job.

But there might be a simpler way. All she had to do was tell Michael her feelings and ask him how he felt about her.

She stood up, his hand in hers, lifted it to her lips and kissed it.

'You know, Michael, I don't always think of you as the boss. Most of the time you're just Michael.'

He didn't say anything, simply wrapped his arms round her and hugged her tightly. The warmth of his body penetrated Kay's thin dress and she breathed in the scent of him. As Michael's mouth met hers, she was aware of voices approaching.

She felt she ought to break away from Michael's embrace, but he was holding her tightly.

It was only when the dog jumped up at them that Michael gently let her go.

'You've done a good job of digging, Michael.'

Mrs Harris beckoned her.

'I've never seen Michael so peaceful. You're good for him.'

'But I still don't really know where I am with him,' Kay confessed, feeling very comfortable with this woman.

'Why not ask him?'

* * *

'Your parents are really nice,' Kay murmured as Michael slowed for traffic lights when they were approaching Blayton. 'I enjoyed my time with them.'

'They like you.' Michael smiled.

As he reached for her hand the lights changed to green and he put the car into gear and drove off.

When they reached the turning for Elm Close, Michael stopped the car, but neither of them made a move to get out.

'Would you walk in the park with me?'

They strolled hand in hand until they found a vacant seat.

'Kay, I . . . '

At the same time, Kay said, 'There's something . . . '

They grinned at each other.

'Ladies first,' he invited.

Feeling nervous, she began.

'Michael, I love you, and I'd like to marry you. How do you feel about that?'

'Oh, my darling, I was wondering how on earth I could ask you the same thing! Almost from the moment I set eyes on you I've loved you. I knew you'd been hurt in the past, and I didn't want to push you into something you weren't ready for.

'I thought it might be too soon for you to fall in love again. When George kept turning up lately, I wondered if you and he might be seeing each other once more, even though I was delighted to hear you confide in your mother that he meant nothing to you.'

'It's true. George does mean nothing to me.'

'I know that now, but I was also desperately worried that the firm was going to fold after that business with Charlie and then the bank. If that had happened, I'd have had nothing to offer you. And you deserve so much.'

Happiness surged through Kay, but she didn't want him to talk any more, not just now.

She took his face in both her hands, and their lips met tenderly before passion propelled them into a deeper embrace.

THE END

We do hope that you have enjoyed reading this large print book.

Did you know that all of our titles are available for purchase?

We publish a wide range of high quality large print books including:
Romances, Mysteries, Classics
General Fiction
Non Fiction and Westerns

Special interest titles available in large print are:
The Little Oxford Dictionary
Music Book, Song Book
Hymn Book, Service Book

Also available from us courtesy of Oxford University Press:
Young Readers' Dictionary
(large print edition)
Young Readers' Thesaurus
(large print edition)

For further information or a free brochure, please contact us at:
Ulverscroft Large Print Books Ltd.,
The Green, Bradgate Road, Anstey,
Leicester, LE7 7FU, England.
Tel: (00 44) **0116 236 4325**
Fax: (00 44) **0116 234 0205**

AN UNEXPECTED ENCOUNTER

Fenella Miller

Miss Victoria Marsh has an unexpected encounter in the church with a handsome, but disagreeable, soldier who is recuperating from a grievous leg injury. Major Toby Highcliff believes himself to be a useless cripple, but meeting Victoria changes everything. Will he be able to keep her safe from the evil that stalks the neighbourhood and convince her he is the ideal man for her?

ANOTHER CHANCE

Rena George

School teacher Rowan Fairlie's life is set to change when Clett Drummond and his two young daughters take on the tenancy of Ballinbrae Farm. Clett insists he's come to the Highlands to help the girls recover from their mother's death, but Rowan suspects there's more to it. And why does her growing friendship with the family so infuriate the new laird, Simon Fraser? Is it simple jealousy — or are the two men linked by some terrible mystery from the past?

REBELLIOUS HEARTS

Susan Udy

Journalist Alice Jordan can't believe her misfortune when she literally bumps into entrepreneur Dominic Falconer. She is running a newspaper campaign to prevent him from destroying an ancient wood in his apparently never-ending pursuit of profit. However, when it becomes clear that local opinion is firmly on his side, Alice decides to go it alone. Someone has to stop him and she is more than ready for the battle. The trouble is — so is Dominic.

PASSAGE OF TIME

Janet Thomas

When charismatic Josh Stephens literally blows into her life, Melanie Treloar finds him a disturbing presence in the hostel she runs in west Cornwall. During his job of assessing some old mining remains Josh discovers a sea cave that holds an intriguing secret. When he is caught in a cliff fall — saving Melanie's niece — it is Melanie who comes to his rescue. Although this puts their relationship on a new level, can they solve the many problems that still remain?